## Praise [illegible] Leonard and Hungry Paul

*[illegible] Sunday Times as one of the*
*[illegible] Novels of the 21st Century*

'[illegible] and already feels [illegible] classic [illegible] absolutely hooked'
[illegible] Man Booker and Costa [illegible] author

'[illegible] beautiful work of art'
[illegible] of the Irish [illegible] of the year

'[illegible] book is as funny as it is wise, as tender [illegible] Rónán Hession [illegible] goes in [illegible] ordinary friendships that might appear [illegible] and [illegible] he finds [illegible] book [illegible]'
[illegible] *New York Times* [illegible]

'[illegible] of a cult classic'
*[illegible] Irish Independent*

'[illegible] quiet contemplative [illegible] debut [illegible]'
*Irish [illegible]*

'[illegible] humorous [illegible]'
[illegible]

'[illegible] exceptional'
*The Guardian*

'[illegible] voice is so distinctive [illegible] it makes [illegible] to fall in love with [illegible] book'
[illegible]

'[illegible] admirable debuts published in [illegible] over the [illegible]'
*[illegible] Ireland*

PANENKA

# PANENKA

by

**PANENKA**

**RÓNÁN HESSION**

SIGNED BY THE AUTHOR

Rónán Hession

Bluemoose

Copyright © Rónán Hession 2021

First published in 2021 by
Bluemoose Books Ltd
25 Sackville Street
Hebden Bridge
West Yorkshire
HX7 7DJ

www.bluemoosebooks.com

All rights reserved
Unauthorised duplication contravenes existing laws

British Library Cataloguing-in-Publication data
A catalogue record for this book is available from the British Library

Hardback 978-1-910422-67-0

Printed and bound in the UK by Short Run Press

This book is dedicated, with love, to my sons,
Thomas and Jacob.

***Panenka****: In football, a penalty technique in which the taker chips the ball artfully into the centre of the goal, counting on the likelihood that the goalkeeper will have dived to either side.*

# Chapter 1: Panenka

His name was Joseph, but for years they had called him Panenka, a name that was his sadness and his story.

These past months, the pressure pain in his head had been coming almost every night, building like an Atlantic wave that roiled within his dreams until it broke and crashed through his sleep, shocking him awake. It manifested as a clamp on his face. Working at bone level, it would spread from the crease between his eyebrows, around the orbits of his pounding eyes and onwards to his jaw, which would stiffen and lock with tension. He called it his Iron Mask. With the palms of his hands pressed against his cheeks, he would run to the bathroom to compress his face against the cool, hard side of the bath, barely relieving the nerves that had mayday signals pulsing through them.

In its own time and on its own terms, the Iron Mask would eventually lift, allowing the last few ripples of pain to subside and returning Panenka to the unclaimed hours somewhere between late night and early morning. Exhausted, he would haul himself up, his legs all fizzy and useless, and limp back to bed, thinking hungrily about the few hours of sleep that remained. Pulling the duvet up as far as his cheek, which bore no bruises or scars, no evidence of the silent violence, he would catch a bubble of thought passing through his mind: was this time worse or the same as the last? Was the pain spreading or different? But he had learned to ignore these questions: the Iron Mask was unknowable in any real sense and beyond any bargaining.

As Panenka lay there on his side, on one of those shipwrecked mornings he had become so used to, his grandson, Arthur, pushed open the bedroom door and climbed into the bed. His weight was not substantial enough to roll Panenka out of the hollow on his side of the mattress, so the child was able to settle himself back-to-back into a familiar arrangement based on body heat. He had often cited his grandfather's indulgence of these visits as a defence against his mother's objections to them – living in a house of adults will sharpen any seven-year-old's advocacy skills to a precocious level.

On finding her son's bed vacant and ruffled, Marie-Thérèse called into Panenka's room without looking: '*Arthur, five more minutes.*'

'I'm bored,' said Arthur to the ceiling once his mother had gone downstairs and out of range. He turned to Panenka and woke him with a nudge to the kidneys. 'Pop – can I wear a tracksuit today?'

'Morning, my friend,' replied Panenka without opening his eyes or moving.

'Everyone's wearing tracksuits. It makes no sense to force kids to wear uniforms with ties. It's the wrong type of clothes.'

'Tracksuits are Tuesday and Thursday.'

'But you don't get into trouble if you wear them other days.' Arthur leaned up on his elbow and turned Panenka's chin towards him.

'Not getting into trouble is not the same as being good,' said Panenka.

'Do I have to wear a tie, then?'

'No tie. I agree with you there. I can't think of a single reason for you to wear a tie. It hardly makes sense for adults to wear them.'

'*Mama*,' roared Arthur. '*I'm not wearing a tie. Pop says I'm allowed.*'

*'Stop shouting!'* called Marie-Thérèse from downstairs, amid the sounds of spoons and bowls. *'If you want to talk to me, come into the same room that I'm in.'*

'Hit the snooze,' said Arthur.

Panenka pressed the top of his grandson's head and they lay there for a few more minutes, Arthur falling back into the carefree rest of a child and Panenka sobering himself after the intensity of the past night.

He pulled the uniform from the wardrobe in Arthur's room and threw the elastic tie back onto the shelf. Laying the clothes out on the bed, he closed all but the top two buttons of the school shirt, leaving those as practice for Arthur to dress himself, each successful effort getting a star on the chore chart.

Panenka gave Arthur a piggyback downstairs to the kitchen, where Marie-Thérèse was wearing the androgynous trouser suit she had just ironed. The name badge on her lapel had limited space and said 'Trainee Manager: Marie.' She had recently taken a promotion at the supermarket where she had worked for several years, going from cashier to a management role that she had been encouraged to apply for. It was a little bit more money but she lost shift allowances, overtime, and the friendship of the women she had worked with on the registers. And so far she was struggling to assert herself with the men in the stockroom. There was something subtly undermining in their frigid co-operation and she could sense their hostility like a draught on her shoulders whenever she swept through to look in on them. But she contained her anxiety and instead projected managerial competence through her perfectionism. She had been taught that 'retail is detail' and was meticulous in her standards, despite knowing that this was a sure way to get called a bitch behind her back. As she sometimes reminded herself, this was all part of getting ahead and taking her life back, even if the small patch of alopecia behind her left ear had begun to worry her. It was easy to hide it now, but if it became any bigger it would surely expose her lack of confidence, or worse, earn her a nickname.

'Here you go Arthur, make sure you don't get it on your uniform,' she said handing him a bowl of porridge with honey in it. 'We'll have to go to school early today – I'm due in for the delivery shift.'

'Don't worry about that,' said Panenka. 'I have a later start today, so I can drop him off at the gates before I go. He's still waking up, I think.'

Arthur was sitting on a beanbag, staring at cartoons, his bowl balanced on his soft belly as he slouched. His hand rested on the remote, having nudged up the volume to drown out the adults' chatter behind him.

'How are you this morning?' she asked, kissing her father on the top of his head. 'I heard you up and about last night. Everything okay?'

'It's those migraines. I'll get it seen to. I feel normal now, like it never happened. Have you had breakfast?'

'I've a banana in my bag. I'd better run – I need to get in before the delivery is done, I have to check everything off.'

'Can't you get someone else to do it – one of the lads?'

'I could, but if there's a mistake it comes out of my pocket. See you later.' Marie-Thérèse stooped down to kiss Arthur, who was engrossed in the screen. 'Be good for Pop now, won't you, buddy,' she said. As she pulled away he caught the back of her neck and hooked her in for a kiss of his own. Arthur preferred dry kisses – wet ones got wiped off with his sleeve.

Panenka sat over his coffee and porridge, half watching the cartoons himself. His cheeks and forehead were clear; no lingering sensations. He had described it as a face migraine to his doctor, who had known him for years, ever since his footballing days had ended. He and the doctor were about the same age and Panenka was not the first man he had examined who had downplayed his health worries. As their families had grown up, they had often chatted informally during routine check-ups, enjoying the type of jokes that men share in private. The doctor was concerned about the headaches but would say little about the condition except that migraines shouldn't feel like iron masks and that Panenka would need a scan. He could wait nine months or else go private, if he could afford it. Panenka had said that there was no big rush and that he didn't mind waiting, embarrassed about declaring his financial situation to an old friend.

'I'll tell you what,' the doctor said. 'There's a Doctor Wolf who's doing a series of short residencies at the hospital. He's a consultant neurosurgeon from Portugal who's an expert in middle-aged men with headaches who follow underachieving football teams, so maybe I can see about getting you a session with him. It's a teaching residency which means there'll be a registrar there – a trainee surgeon who's learning from him. Would that be a problem?'

'Is that private or public?'

'Neither. It's sort of off-books. It's a teaching consultation so there's no cost, provided you're comfortable with being part of the training process. To be honest, I'm only telling you about this because we've known each other a long time and I think it's worth getting this checked out soon. I don't want to worry you, but I think you need to be examined by someone experienced. It might be nothing, but a nothing from Doctor Wolf is worth more than a nothing from me. Deal?' he asked.

'Why not.'

He had been booked for a preliminary scan the following week, getting an afternoon off work to go on his own. It was all over in time for him to be home for dinner with Marie-Thérèse and Arthur at the usual hour. He had said nothing to them about the scan or the panic attack that he had when he was in the MRI scanner, nor about the long chat with the young radiographer about changing his mind, or the submissive resignation when he was delivered into the machine for a second time, feeling utterly powerless and alone. He had expected that they would print off the scan pictures like at a passport booth, and tell him the news one way or the other. But the pictures had to be referred to Doctor Wolf and Doctor Nunes, whoever he was, or, as it turned out, whoever she was. It had taken four weeks for Doctor Wolf's office to call Panenka for that morning's appointment.

Panenka shaped the last few lumps of porridge into a spoonful and finished it.

'Time's up, Arthur. Brush your teeth before it's too late. We're going in 300 seconds.'

'That's five minutes,' said Arthur without shifting. He was used to his grandfather's sly way of pushing arithmetic on him.

They walked through the part of town Panenka had lived in for many years, an area known as the Crucible, where a mix of strays, seasonal workers and outsider communities lived; people dependent on the local authorities, mostly. Over the years, much of the area had been scheduled for demolition – or urban regeneration as it was called – but there was always a new population of unwanted people who needed to be housed somewhere, anywhere, and the Crucible served a useful purpose as far as the town was concerned. It was a sort of spare room where all the problems were dumped with a view to sorting them out later, or forgetting about them altogether. It was where the pavements crumbled, where blown streetlamps went the longest without being fixed, where people used sheets as curtains, where grown men lived four to a room in bunk beds. For all its flaws, it was cheap and within walking distance of most places. Panenka had always liked the invisibility of living in the Crucible, it being full of people from elsewhere who were too busy with their own precarious lives to notice him.

They walked up to the school with Panenka shouldering Arthur's bag, which was heavier than he had expected. In it was a Tupperware box packed with the 'school bismuth,' a futuristic silver-grey block from the science table that Arthur had been entrusted with over the weekend as a reward for coming second in a quiz. It had never left his bag.

'Pop – what's plastic surgery?' asked Arthur, kicking a flattened Coke can into the road while they waited at a pedestrian crossing.

'It's when people get an operation on their skin to make them look younger. It flattens out their wrinkles.'

'Oh.'

'Why? What did you think it was?'

'I don't know. I thought it was like *pretend* surgery.'

'Come on, it's a green man.'

'Mama says that some people are addicted to plastic surgery.'

'Let's not talk crossing the road, my friend. Wait until we get to the other side. Remember, both ways.'

'I'm doing it.'

'Don't be a lighthouse, moving your head from side to side. Pay attention.'

At the other kerb they joined the shoal of children holding hands with grown-ups, all going in the same direction.

'Do footballers get plastic surgery?'

'Not when I played. These days they look like pop stars, so maybe that's changed. I was more worried about surgery on my knees or my ankles.'

'Did you ever have an operation?'

'A few times, unfortunately.'

'What was the worst one?'

'Once I broke my leg and then they had to break it again because it didn't set properly.'

'That's disgusting.'

Arthur grabbed his bag when they reached the school gates and bolted to join a group of boys who were huddled and talking excitedly like Wall Street traders. He had quietly explained to Panenka a few weeks before that goodbye kisses were acceptable at home but not in public. Even hugs and high fives were being suspended pending a full review. Arthur was comparing heights with a boy that Panenka had seen before at one of the birthday parties. Arthur looked cleaner and newer standing next to him, with hair that was styled and not just short. His shoes didn't have broken laces. His jumper was fitted without looking too small. The other boy looked a little unfinished beside him, not that either of them noticed or cared. It all came from Marie-Thérèse and her unappreciated attention to the little things. She kept it all in her head. All on top of her new job and the thousand-and-one other things a twenty-eight-year-old mother was supposed to fit into her life.

The school bell rang and the children ran screaming into their lines as the parents broke off their small talk and dispersed back to their cars: mostly mothers, a few dads and, least hassled of all, the grandparents helping out. At fifty, Panenka was a young grandfather and was good at it – that is to say, interested in it. There was a playful inversion involved in the grandfather/grandson relationship. It was child-led. Arthur chose the agenda and set the pace for their conversations, which always led back to him answering his own questions in his own way. He had such an innocent certainty, as though he were not so much figuring things out as recalling lost knowledge from a previous existence. Working methodically, he used yes/no questions to deconstruct the world's inconsistencies and injustices. In all this Panenka was the sidekick – the 'who's there?' in the knock-knock joke, as well as the clown, the tickler, the absurdist, the dumb bunny that Arthur explained things to. Nobody ever goes to counselling about their difficult grandparents. It is love without the stakes. If only Panenka's other relationships had been like that. Perhaps they could have been. But it was too late for that thought. It was needed years ago, when he was failing as a father, a husband, a friend, and as a human. Too much of his life had involved making mistakes that carved deep grooves into the lives of those around him. Who was he to be wise now? He had always guessed that his bad choices would have to be accounted for eventually and that there would be a reckoning. So that was how he saw things, and that was how he saw the abjection of the night and the bathroom floor.

# Chapter 2: Doctor Wolf

The appointment was in a part of the hospital that Panenka had never been to before – a sort of annexe-to-an-annexe, where he presumed the doctors received their training and where the famous administrative machinery of the health service was housed. There were no trolleys or people in pyjamas, and the feeling of sickness was missing from the corridors, but it still felt like a place where life-changing things happened. He found the waiting room by asking a porter and showing him the appointment letter, pointing like a tourist with no language skills. The porter swiped him through a series of double doors and brought him to a reception desk where the formalities were mercifully brief, the appointment letter doubling as a passport through the bureaucracy.

Looking around the waiting room at the other patients, he soon understood what it took to earn an appointment with Doctor Wolf. These were the hard cases. The extreme, the statistically improbable, the researchable, peer-reviewable, seen-once-in-your-career, educational-for-a-reason cases. A man with buck teeth and stubble sat reading a tabloid with a lump the size of a billiard ball at his temple. An undersized child – could even have been a teenager – sat punching his own head and trying to pull out tufts of hair, his mother beside him so used to this that she batted his hand down without even lifting her eyes from her phone. A blind woman in her forties sat with her husband, holding his hand, her speech sounding drunken and slow. A beautiful young woman, into punk by the looks of it, was locked into intermittent spasms that whiplashed her head backwards every few minutes, her dad keeping his hand behind her head to stop it cracking off the wall behind. And there sat Panenka among them, the only patient with nobody to accompany him.

He took his seat and started worrying properly. It was one thing to indulge the hope of denial about his own health, but to be grouped and classified in such company told him where the doctors' weighted probabilities placed him. Panenka could hardly bear to look at them. Had his doctor called in a favour to get him an appointment, or had the Iron Mask got him there? Had the great Doctor Wolf pulled his file personally from a hundred others, a winner in the triage lottery because of the obscurity and desperation of his condition? Was he there to be helped, or was he beyond help and instead picked to donate his poor fortune to the advancement of medical understanding?

A young female doctor came out of the office and called the name of Jonathan somebody. The boy who had been pulling out his hair stood up and was guided by his mother into the office, his eyesight obviously affected by whatever condition he had. When they came out afterwards their faces were stony and unlit. Maybe there were some problems that even Doctor Wolf couldn't take on. Each patient was invited in turn by the young doctor Panenka assumed was Doctor Nunes, and emerged a short time later to convey their own story to the waiting patients through little more than body language and eyes haunted with imminent crying.

Panenka was the only one left and had begun to wonder whether Doctor Wolf had run out of time or had perhaps already decided that the morning had provided enough grim education for any registrar. But eventually Doctor Nunes called him in, reading his name from the front of a manila file and offering a smile as he identified himself to her.

'Thank you for your patience. I'm the registrar who'll be sitting in on your consultation with Doctor Wolf. I'm sorry about the delay but we have to overbook, as a lot of patients drop out. It's not ideal, but it means we can see and help as many people as possible.'

She was about the same age as Marie-Thérèse and had that same air of professionalism about her – another young person who had already assumed an unfair share of life's responsibility. He didn't know how people did it.

Panenka had had plenty of time to imagine what Doctor Wolf would be like. Initially he had assumed a mature, portly man who would be all professorial alpha masculinity. But the parade of broken souls that he had seen leaving the office had changed his mind: he now expected an officer's side parting and the dead eyes of an overachieving careerist. In his days as a professional footballer with Seneca FC, he had always dealt with club doctors who treated the players with the kind of care and respect that any valuable company asset deserved. Several of them were obviously hired as part of the performance drugs culture that was prevalent in football back then. They travelled from club to club with the same coaches, achieving miraculous injury recovery times and passing the supposedly random tests required by the National Football Association. He had never got involved in that, not for moral reasons but because he had never been trusted enough by his club to be asked to cheat.

Panenka sat in the chair that Doctor Nunes gestured towards. Doctor Wolf was looking at the scan results on a computer and didn't acknowledge his presence. He had a thin, veiny face, with grey bushy hair around his ears and a comb-over that gave up halfway across his scalp. Doctor Wolf asked his younger colleague a brief question in what Panenka recognised as Portuguese. Panenka had once partnered in midfield with a rangy Brazilian workhorse named Erasmo who bantered during games in street Portuguese, but he no longer had an ear for the language and had to read the doctors by their faces instead. As they discussed the file, Doctor Nunes seemed to be getting defensive – whatever Doctor Wolf had said, it had included a note of reprimand, which was now passed on to Panenka in turn.

'Who did you bring with you?' she asked.

'How do you mean?'

'The letter you got from the clinic, have you got it with you?'

'Sure, here.'

'No, don't give it to *me*,' she snapped, impatience leaking through her strained professionalism. 'Tell me what it says at the bottom in bold and underlined text.'

'*Please ensure that you are accompanied by a partner, friend or family member*. Okay, so?'

'Okay, so,' she said curtly. 'Where is your partner, friend or family member?'

Panenka absorbed the provocation, unsure how to interpret it. Prickly humiliation surged inside him but hit a trip switch.

She released Panenka's stolid stare and relayed the gist of things to Doctor Wolf, leading to a testy back and forth between them, the older doctor repeating a phrase in slow, patronising syllables, adding his own bold and underline by way of an index finger tapping at the screen. Doctor Nunes seemed accustomed to being spoken to that way.

'This is important, all right?' she said, turning back to Panenka, her tone softened, her manner regathered in preamble to seriousness.

Carefully, Doctor Wolf conveyed in single clauses, each of which was translated in turn by Doctor Nunes, information of a technical-sounding neutrality utterly at odds with its import. He spoke about a nut-sized tumour, whose novelty lay in its position, shape, intractability and the risks it posed, risks that the doctor could take but which were really Panenka's to own; risks that could be for life, and other risks that did not admit the language of life. While the doctors spoke in turn, as if reciting wedding vows, Panenka strayed into a stunned reverie: a protective daydream populated with ghosts from a life past, barely present, and perhaps, now, never to come. He realised that all through those long nights under the Iron Mask, there had been a knowing – his body had been trying to make him understand that it was betraying him. There had begun a peeling away of identity. The Panenka in the mirror, in photographs, in football sticker albums, in match day programmes, and in others' memories of him, was separating from itself. The bodily Panenka was being isolated, while some other, more subtle, Panenka looked on.

The doctors were exact in their use of words, words that passed through him, all about options that weren't really options. In the end, it was a Hippocratic judgement that nothing could or should be done. A decision not to intervene was often the hardest, Doctor Wolf explained vicariously – perhaps more for his younger colleague's benefit – and it takes many years of experience for a surgeon to learn when to make it.

It had been the briefest of exchanges about some of life's most important truths, in which poetry and philosophy had given way to bald practicality. When asked whether he had understood everything, Panenka breathed a quiet 'yes.' He would not, after all, be visited by the luck he had gone so much of his life without.

'I'm very sorry,' said Doctor Wolf, addressing Panenka directly for the first time.

Panenka felt that counterfeit calm of bad news, the withdrawal of feeling before it crashes back in later with the full force of realisation. His shoes squeaked on the corridor afterwards as he stuffed the obsolete letter into his pocket, walking against the flow of other people, separated from them by what he now knew. The Iron Mask would eventually prevail, however long that took; his only question was how he should live until then.

# Chapter 3: Marie-Thérèse

'Say something encouraging,' said Marie-Thérèse.

'Like what?' said Carla.

She had known Carla for years, and it was a testament to their friendship that it had even survived the end of Marie-Thérèse's social life after she became a young parent. It was Carla's job to keep Marie-Thérèse sane and grounded, a task to which her temperament and outlook were well suited.

'Anything. Something that will make me feel less like one of the bad people in the world.'

'You have nice skin – creamy.'

'Not that sort of stuff.'

'What's the problem? So you got in trouble at work. I've had loads of "chats" with my boss. It's actually an alternative to them being properly pissed off and having a go at you.'

'Yeah, but for as long as I've known you you've always been in trouble: school, rows with your family and all that. Trouble is who you are.'

'Even though it's true, it doesn't mean you have to say it out loud. It has to be helpful and the other person has to be ready to hear it.'

'Very profound, Carla.'

'It's something they told us on a training course at work about how to give feedback to someone you're planning to sack. Maybe I should collect all these things and write a book.'

'Please don't. I need people who stay with me on earth. Everyone I have to deal with these days is either a dreamer or a big thinker. What you have, Carla, never gets old.'

'I can never tell whether you're complimenting me. I mean, it sounds like a compliment, but there's this little twist in it that makes me wonder.'

'I hate the way that I do a thousand things right and end up getting hassle because of one mistake – it's not even a mistake, more a miscalculation. A slight adjustment this way or that and it would have been fine.'

'What happened exactly?' asked Carla.

They were having this discussion late in the evening at the kitchen table, on the hard chairs. This was the forum for sorting things out. Idle, meandering conversations were held on the couch, but showdown discussions and all things problematic were brought to the table.

'I had them facing off, you know, packing the shelves and straightening the produce on display, and they were all in and out to the stockroom like sparrows at a bird feeder. Instead of bringing out pallets and doing it properly, they were nipping in there and carrying boxes and armfuls, so I pulled one of them up on it and he stares at me and nods. Then it occurs to me that he's got food in his mouth, so I call him back and ask him straight out: "Are you eating something?" And he gives me this facial reaction, like "Woah, what's this?" so I repeat myself. He shakes his head. At this stage we both know he's raided the stores and has a snack or something in his mouth. Then I do the whole, "I'm going to give you a chance to tell me the truth ..." but he walks off and ignores me calling him. I'm furious and go to look for another manager to act as witness, but next thing he's back with this other guy, who is this prize, ugh, I won't even go there. But as I was saying, this other guy, from the union, who thinks he's Nelson Mandela, starts accusing me of instigating body searches, of demonising the staff, of making false *criminal* accusations, of intimidation, bullying et cetera. He wants to lodge a complaint, which he knows means going over my head to my manager, and that's the bit that gets me. It's not even about the complaint: it's about how they contrive to exclude me so that they can straighten it out with my boss. It's their way of showing that they can bypass me any time they like.'

'What did your boss say to them?'

'I've no idea. All he said was that it's sorted and I shouldn't worry – these things are all about process. But for all I know he said to them "Look lads, she's new, she's finding her feet. Give her a chance." All that rubbish. Who knows how he might have sold me out?'

'I thought you said he was all right? He more or less picked you for the job didn't he?'

'He sort of did, yeah. I'm not sure what to make of him. He said to me the other day, "Look, figure out how you want to run this shift, and I'll back whatever you decide." I don't know whether he's being empowering or lazy, knowing I'll work hard and intercept all the grief that's intended for him.'

Marie-Thérèse could see that she was boring Carla a little bit.

'Sorry, I know you don't know these people. I probably sound a bit defensive.'

'Some jobs are so bad that you have to pay people to do them.'

'That's another one for your book. Enough about my struggles, how's your job going?'

'People ring in, I give them quotes, send them letters about their no claims bonus, people complain about their premiums and tell me they can do better elsewhere and then they come back and renew anyway. I'm living the dream. The big thing now is data protection, but to be honest I'm not in the mood for work talk. Why don't we go out at the weekend – have a few drinks, nothing too crazy. I can get the girls out and we can do it properly.'

'Sounds nice, though whenever I think about going out I end up wondering where all my energy has gone. All I can think of is the effort – what's happening to me? Promise me you won't let me turn into an old lady, will you?'

'Don't start with the excuses. All you have to do is look forward to it and enjoy it when you're out. Get Vincent to take Arthur for a sleepover.'

'He has his place to look after on weekend nights, which means he can't get off – he takes Arthur on Mondays or Wednesdays – like, what am I supposed to do on a Monday night? Maybe my dad can babysit – I'll ask him.'

Marie-Thérèse paused for a few beats and then lifted up the hair behind her left ear to reveal a small patch of alopecia.

'Could you measure it for me?'

'Sure, let me see. How big was it?'

'Size of a stamp you said.'

'Well, it's a little bit bigger, but not by much.'

Marie-Thérèse mouthed a single but effective expletive.

'*Mama – I need a drink of water*,' called Arthur from his bed upstairs. '*I really need it*.'

'*Coming up now*,' she called back. 'Give me a minute, he usually settles again quickly.' Marie-Thérèse pushed off the table to lift herself up.

'Call it a bad day. Start again tomorrow,' said Carla, picking up the remote, and moving to the couch.

Upstairs, Arthur was sitting at the edge of his bed. He was panting melodramatically as Marie-Thérèse brought him his mug of water, which he chugged back, leaving himself breathless. His hair was damp with sweat so she opened his window a crack.

'Don't let any bugs in,' he said.

'They won't come in as long as your lights are off,' she said. 'Did you have a bad dream?'

'I don't have dreams. I was only asleep for a second.'

'Hop back in there now and I'll tuck your quilt in.'

'Can you come in beside me?'

'I have my friend Carla downstairs. She'll be lonely if I stay up here too long.'

'Ten minutes?'

'Five.'

'Seven?'

'Scootch over then.'

She lay down beside him, the edge of her body leaning out of the bed.

'Can I have the waves?'

'We're fine like this, buddy. You don't need the waves.'

'The waves help me sleep. I *need* them.'

Marie-Thérèse went into her room to get her little egg-shaped speaker. Arthur took the phone from her and scrolled with his pudgy thumb until he got the wave sounds and settled down with the phone resting on his chest.

'Go to sleep now, little man.'

She lay back on the pillow as he linked his arm through hers, like an old married couple. Her feet were tingling and her mind, too tired for thought, started to release its grip on the day. The energy lifted from her body like a ghost. She stared at the stippled ceiling above her, an acned constellation of petrified drips. Her tongue came to rest on the roof of her mouth, as Arthur's arm slipped from hers, or maybe it was hers that slipped from his. Fully dressed, she dissolved into sleep, waking hours after Carla had already let herself out.

# Chapter 4: Vincent's

The sign outside Vincent's said 'Café-Bar' with the implication being that it was positioned somewhere on a rich spectrum between those two possibilities. It was located on a back street near the edge of the Crucible, a street whose main virtue was that it was a shortcut to other more interesting streets. Though the café-bar had wide frontage, with windows that began at waist height and spanned the full panorama from left to right, it had the wrong orientation for attracting sunlight, which seldom made it past the threshold. Vincent's was popular, if that was the word, as a place of conversation for patrons who didn't spend much money and who could make a single drink last as long as any given argument.

Its previous owner had managed it according to strict standards of parsimony, making a virtue of inertia, citing his commitment to preserving the town's traditional café culture. To him, this was the headquarters of the old town, terminology that appeared in no guide book or tourist information but which abounded in the elaborate narratives he spun to fictionalise the failing business he was looking to sell. He ran it, and ran it down, over a period of thirty years or more, during which he never missed a rent payment and never made an improvement he could avoid. It was furnished with every expense spared and, though the customers were not hugely opinionated about things like decor and design, there was an oppressive feeling of bachelorhood about the place: not the rollicking, free-living kind, but an economising self-neglect.

That was around the time that Marie-Thérèse had separated from her husband Vincent, who was out of work and needed something to do. Vincent accepted a loan from Panenka to secure the lease in the hope that he could make the arrangement a long-term one. Though Vincent was traditional in outlook and believed in the immutability of the marriage contract – in that two people got married as they were, sold as seen – he was not inflexible. He saw that commitment meant it was possible to have distance without discord. To him love was no union between two otherwise incomplete halves, but more like the gravity that locked two bodies into the same orbit, each doing their own thing but by reference to and in concert with the other. If Marie-Thérèse disappeared to the dark side of the moon once in a while, it was wiser to trust her return to the natural course of their relationship rather than give chase and risk a collision. During this separation the café-bar had come to stand for his place in the world, his counterfactual self: the person he was when he was without Marie-Thérèse. He calculated that its success and the future it offered their family – and what it spoke about him – was his best hope of exerting the necessary forces that might bring her back.

With all this at stake, Vincent began making big plans for the modernisation of the place. He would sometimes test his ideas on the small parliament of regular customers who usually agreed to hear him out. After much reflection and discussion, they would eventually come to a view that, if it were any nearer to the point, could almost be called an opinion. 'If you want a quick answer,' they would say, 'it is No. But if you are prepared to wait, then the answer might not be No.' It was disheartening for Vincent to learn that politics was not limited to the home but also pervaded the workplace. He was naturally non-confrontational and it daunted him to face into a draining sequence of coaxing and bargaining, compromise and deal making. With his customers, it could be hard to say what they wanted exactly, or whether they disagreed at all, and even if they did, what the cause of concern or source of satisfaction might be specifically. Their opinions were like a gas that pervaded everything, but which never settled in any one place.

Apart from Panenka, Vincent's regulars included Anthony, BABA and, in recent months, Teddy.

Anthony's marriage was not merely unhappy, but sorrowful. Each night he went home to a wife who lay in bed with her back to him, silent or else weeping, and who did not acknowledge his returns, just as she did not acknowledge his departures. With no precipitating event or miscommunication to explain how this situation had come to be, he was shadowed throughout his days by the unexplained melancholy in his soul partner. He had worshipped her long brown hair, which used to settle in the hollow of her back, but she had cut it on the day that the sadness arrived. With her back turned, he could see the graduated crop and the bare nape of her neck, her ears protruding and boy-like.

Then there was BABA, who liked to sit at the bar and read instead of joining the others. It was his style to overhear rather than listen, to interject rather than participate. He disliked it when others trespassed beyond their learning and was quick to highlight that he had two Bachelor of Arts degrees, an achievement which had earned him his nickname, even though it was often pointed out by Anthony that an honours degree was a progression from a pass degree, and not a second qualification in its own right.

There had been a recent and temporary addition to the staff in the form of Teddy, a young man who had started at Vincent's on work experience as part of a government scheme. He was hired as a factotum to help with the food orders, though the menu was limited to a daily one-pot dish, misnomered the 'special.' The kitchen closed at eight but was seldom busy after lunch, so once the cleaning and prep for the next day was done, Teddy liked to join the conversation and enjoy the one free drink daily that Vincent had agreed to in the name of industrial relations. He was not paid much, simply receiving a top up to his unemployment benefit during a six month placement where he was to learn knife skills, team-building, poultry handling and punctuality. At a guess, he was about nineteen or twenty and was still growing. With his willowy body, he looked more like a small man who had been stretched rather than a man who was tall per se.

Panenka arrived at Vincent's that evening having spent the day in an ambulatory trance after the morning's appointment, which had left him with so much to weigh. By now the doctors would be at home with their families or meeting friends or otherwise finding a response to the question about how their day had gone, and in that human way would reach for an answer they could live with. But Panenka, not yet sure how to drag his bad news into the house, first sought to restore himself in the society of other men. At least Vincent's was a familiar place, where he could feel at ease among those who accepted the existence of back stories and unseen lives that did not belong at the café-bar. There was a safety in that, and perhaps also a tacit contract.

He found his friends quorate and on the upward arc of debate. The topic, sponsored by Vincent, was the erection of a mounted TV to watch football.

'What's the big deal?' asked Vincent. 'For the first time in years Seneca has the chance to return to top-tier football and the town is starting to get behind them again. Why can't we be part of that buzz – show the games in the run-in, and then next year we'll be playing all the top clubs. It'll be like the classic days.'

'They'll soon learn,' said Anthony. 'Seneca is a team that teaches philosophy. The town will be like a flat glass of lemonade in a couple of weeks. We've been through this before. If ever there was a club that traded on disappointment, it was Seneca.'

'That's not true. We've had good cup runs – up to semi-finals twice in my lifetime,' countered Vincent.

'Exactly,' said Anthony. 'We are a semi-final type of club. You can't disappoint people without getting their hopes up first. If we were bad all the time it would be fine, but it's the whole pattern of taking the odd big scalp, or miraculously finding a gifted player, and then settling back into our usual apathetic form. Following Seneca is an endurance sport that never ends.'

'It's not only about TV,' said BABA, without looking up from his book. 'A place has to have ambience, mood. When you change things you can lose all that, and it's not easy to restore it once you do. All the conversations held in this room get baked into its furnishings. You shouldn't rush into disturbing all that.'

'Look, if I don't get more customers there won't be anywhere for you to bake your conversations, that's all I'm saying,' said Vincent. 'And there's a bit too much mood in this carpet if you ask me. Nothing gets it out. No wonder we don't get any women coming in. I wouldn't bring Marie-Thérèse in here, or Arthur. Wouldn't it be nice to have more of a family feeling about the place? Or maybe we could become an affiliated place for supporters.'

'Those people are drinkers,' said Anthony. 'Football is their excuse for drinking. Every big game is an excuse for drinking, as is every celebration and disappointment. If that's the type of customer you're looking for then say so, because I don't see why you're asking us about becoming a sports bar.'

'No, not exactly, I was thinking more of a family, football, *and* conversation, type place,' said Vincent struggling to put a shape on his proposition. 'And would it be such a bad idea if we had a few female customers?'

'You people are afraid of women,' said BABA, taking off his glasses and resting his book on the bar. The debate was now sufficiently mature for him to consider it worthy of being addressed directly. 'I listen to your discussions—'

'How gracious of you!' interjected Anthony.

'—and you forget that this man here needs to run a business. This isn't free day care. I myself am not a football fan and I don't watch TV. But I could find another quiet place somewhere else in this town if it all became too much. I don't expect Vincent to take care of me in my old age.'

'Who else would have you?' said Anthony.

'I would have no trouble finding a welcome in any number of other places,' replied BABA.

'I see. Yet no names come to mind immediately.'

'I am not trying to persuade you, Anthony. I am merely answering your question,' said BABA.

BABA returned to his book, the essays of Michel de Montaigne, which he had been reading for several years now. The others were not big readers and generally assumed that BABA's interventions had some basis in Montaigne himself.

'Look,' said Vincent, the peacemaker. 'I'm not planning to kick any of you out or replace you. I wouldn't be asking your opinion if I didn't care what you thought. Think of it as something to reflect on. I would like to see this place a bit fuller – I can't ignore the commercial side of things.'

Panenka, who had spent the day in unleavened seriousness, found consolation in this patter, as he so often did. He had learned all about the wisdom of levity, even as Anthony reported on the funeral of his old boss.

'So what happened to him in the end?' asked Teddy.

'Oh, well he died while trying to demolish his shed from the inside with a lump hammer – the roof caved in on his head.'

'The poor man,' said Teddy. 'Why didn't he attack it from the outside?'

'Well, obviously that would have been better,' said Anthony. 'The evidence speaks for itself.'

'Sounds like he wasn't the type of man who thought things through,' suggested BABA.

'He was like that all his life,' said Anthony. 'He used to buy old classic cars and do them up in his back garden – Saabs mostly. He'd spend months and months working on them – they'd be up on bricks for ages, waiting for parts. He had this old 900 turbo that he was working on and had to wait to find a set of reconditioned brake callipers – the handbrake worked on the front wheels on those ones, I had one myself, parts were always hard to get. But in the meantime he had built an extension onto the side of his house – a downstairs toilet for his wife who couldn't climb stairs after her accident. By the time the car was ready he couldn't get it out.'

'He should have moved it out before he did the extension,' offered Teddy.

'Again, I agree with you, and I'm sure that, in retrospect so would he,' said Anthony.

'What did he do then?' asked the young man.

'What could he do?' said Anthony. 'He buried it. It's still there, I'd say.'

Teddy threw down his ripped beer mat at the very thought of it.

The evening played out as it always did, like a non-recurring decimal, each thought causing the next, onwards without resolution. After it had wound down, Anthony lifted his coat and made to leave and Panenka, his mood softened, joined him. They chatted while walking part of the way together.

'You were quiet tonight,' observed Anthony.

'Enjoying the company too much. I did a bit of walking today; must have tired myself out. How are things at home?'

'No change. She seems to lie awake all the time. I brought her some tea and toast in bed this morning, but I got no reaction. The poor lamb is exhausted. I came in from work and she was still in bed, lying on her side, the toast uneaten on her bedside table. I don't know if she's starving herself or what.'

'Have you tried doctors and all that?'

'She wouldn't go. Eventually I got the doctor to call to our house. She cooperated with him, but he couldn't do anything for her. I asked him, I said, "Is she depressed or what?" but he said it was hard to say for sure. So we go through the same thing every day.'

'Any idea what's behind it?'

'No. I can only hope it's one of those things that goes away after a while. But it's hard not to think that it's something I have done or said – or not done or not said. After all, I'm her husband. I thought we were close.'

They stood for a moment before parting, the conversation stuck at that unfinishable thought.

The lights were on when Panenka opened the front door at home. There was a general feeling of abandonment about the place. He picked up the shoes lying around and tidied away the wine glasses. Upstairs he found Marie-Thérèse asleep in Arthur's bed, but decided not to wake her in case he disturbed Arthur, whose limbs were wrapped around hers.

He had thought his days of hurting those he loved were behind him, but when had he ever been able to promise that?

# Chapter 5: Seneca FC

The excitement about Seneca FC's possible promotion to the top division for the first time in a generation was palpable around a town that had little else going for it. It was an insular club of local heroes who enjoyed a degree of hometown adoration that was utterly at odds with their reputation in the wider footballing world. When Panenka was growing up, before Seneca's decline, home matches sold out and season tickets were bought in family batches. Factory floor banter was not between rival fans, but between different shades of fan, each of whom wanted what was best for the club, whatever their personal definition of that was. No two Seneca fans were alike, as their arguments proved. Any young player with potential would be given the opportunity to have a trial when they came of age, and rejection letters were framed and hung in kitchens around the town. The club's academy taught young players to develop themselves not only as footballers but as people, instilling in them what it saw as the primary agent of human fulfilment: self-respect. First team players were expected to live in the town and shop in its shops. They signed whatever jerseys or programmes were presented to them and could be seen posing for photographs with fans who stopped them in the streets. Seneca preferred home-grown players. Transfer market dealings were undertaken begrudgingly and with anxiety about protecting its ethos. It was a sentimental and antiquated approach that had been instrumental in the club's descent down the divisions in recent times.

It was not difficult for Seneca to hear about new prospects. In a one-team town obsessed with the club, nothing was missed. Scouts were well known and picked up every scrap of news from the dozens of feeder clubs playing in the youth leagues. They were inscrutable, perspicacious souls who could cause panic in a team by showing up unannounced only to leave early. The players would forget about the day's result and instead discuss the scout's behaviour obsessively. Did he take notes? Did anyone get a call after last Saturday's match? Why did he have to show up on the week that I was being played out of position? Could he not have waited and come when my hamstring had recovered? What if he never returns?

Panenka had just turned seventeen and had been monitored for several games without realising it, the scouts themselves having scouts who did the initial reconnaissance before any more open declaration of interest was made. None of this spooked him – he knew that he would be watched eventually. There were many specific things that a scout would look for and assess, but chief among them was whether a young player already looked and carried himself like a first team footballer. There was an uncommon maturity in his play, a confidence in his choices, and a charismatic aggression that communicated itself on the pitch and to everyone watching.

When he was eventually called for his trial, a few of the young players involved took photos around the Seneca complex, as though they were tourists who didn't deserve to be there and who didn't expect to be back. Others were nervous and it showed in how they talked too much, the novelty overwhelming them. But Panenka had always been able to access some secret pocket of cold focus within him whenever he needed it. There was no emotional crescendo, simply the clear certainty that he belonged at the club. He went there determined not to be satisfied with a trial, but to become important in its history.

It was around then that he met Lauren. He was out with a group of friends, getting used to the privileges of a footballer's life when it came to women, and Lauren was sitting at the edge of the conversation, obviously bored, like someone waiting for a rain shower to pass. His competitive side wanted to overcome her lack of interest in him, so he radiated attention towards her, directing his best lines her way and hoping to tease from her some small victory by way of a reaction. When the others moved on to a nightclub she said she would pass, not for want of being a good sport, but because of what Panenka would come to know as her incorruptible self-sufficiency. Her first answer was always her real answer and she didn't need anyone to talk her into or out of things. So, she stayed behind and he, all but declaring instant loyalty, stayed with her.

Lauren had grown up locally, but to her Seneca was something abstract: its colours, its history, its romance, its hold on the town, were all things she viewed with scepticism. As far as she was concerned, the club was merely the owner of the town's tallest building, and football was something that offered an identity to people who didn't have one of their own. The town was a small place in every respect and she had that youthful sense of the possibilities of elsewhere. Once she could get enough money together her plan was to travel, and the town would become part of her past. She shared all this in that cavalier spirit of one who was done investing in her present life, offloading her thoughts like last year's school books. But perhaps that was what led her to open up so carelessly to Panenka in the weeks that followed. Love does its work by mingling two people. Without realising it, by letting him in she had accidentally changed her life and her plans. It would be a long time before Lauren got the chance to leave and by then she would be a different person.

Panenka spent the first few seasons on apprentice wages in the youth team – often out of position and out of form – before being given a second chance in a loan move to a smaller club two hours' drive away, for which he had to borrow Lauren's car and the petrol she put in it. He soon discovered that lower league football had developed an answer to young players suspected of having notions of superiority, and that referees played their own part in this hazing. Studs ploughed down his calves and his purple ribs ached in the showers after games. The stick that Panenka got on the pitch was matched by his treatment in the dressing room. The older players, in particular those who would never have the chance to play top level football, had seen many loan moves like Panenka's over the years: young prospects from big clubs who got sent to grow up in the lower leagues among those who belonged there. It was a model that had proved successful in breaking many young players, though it was less successful at putting them back together again. It was a miserable time for him, full of doubt and disappointment, injury and exhaustion. His confidence had spoiled, and in a sport where self-belief is the animating force for everything that comes after it, he felt like a ghost on the pitch. Worst of all was the abuse from the supporters who had decided, in that way crowds have of reaching consensus quickly and fervently, that he lacked not only experience, which was forgivable, but commitment, which was not. The long drives back from matches gave him time to listen to the criticism on local radio, where he was discussed as one-dimensional and out of his depth. Lauren, whose reasons for not watching football had changed during those years from there being too little at stake to there being too much, never came to see him play. But whenever he arrived home to the tiny flat they were renting and saw the table laid with the take-away and cheap wine she had somehow budgeted for, he knew that she had heard everything.

# Chapter 6: Night Thoughts

Ever since the hospital appointment, Panenka's late night punishments under the Iron Mask had become more sadistic and his ability to cope with them even more depleted. The pain was compounded by sleep deprivation and exhaustion, physical states unmatched in their ability to summon dangerous emotional forces.

For days his mind had been revisiting the same concern over and over, like a tongue worrying a bad tooth. Panenka was a deeply private person. Those who knew him knew to accept his inscrutable habits: late night walks through the town's closed-up streets; long shift hours doing God-knows-what God-knows-where; unexplained absences; early rising and late returning. Years of life untraced and unshared. He had told nobody about the Iron Mask or about his intention to retreat like a woodland animal and deal with it alone. But illness meant dependency. It was society's last chance to push the benefits of membership. For every person who feared dying alone, there were others like Panenka who resisted the intimacy of it, the body's loss of privacy and the final exhibition of the personality.

The night, with all its questions, called for a full audit of his closest and oldest relationships, in which the ledger recorded that those who had loved him most had lost the most. The only thing he wanted from life now was a settlement, and the time in which to make it.

Above all, he wanted to avoid the burden falling on Marie-Thérèse. Panenka's fatherhood had been mixed up in the saddest times of his life. After he had left Seneca in ignominy as a young man, he had entered a selfish period of survival, one which had been at the expense of his daughter, who was three at the time, and her mother, Lauren, Panenka's ex-wife. They had rained love on him, willing him to open up and accept their support, but it all bounced back off the carapace that had formed around his wounded inner self. The tragedy during that time was that he neither let them in nor let them go. But what else is possible for a man unable to solve his own sadness?

Somehow Marie-Thérèse had found her way back to him when she was in her twenties. Undamaged and ungrudging, she had grown into a confident young woman and reasserted her role as daughter, setting aside what was unanswered from their elliptical history. When her marriage to Vincent began to unspool, he invited her to stay with him for as long as she needed. Panenka had since come to recognise his time with Arthur and Marie-Thérèse as a precious and undeserved second chance to experience a family from the inside. He had promised himself that he would never again hurt those he loved. Having been rescued, he didn't want to be the drowning man who pulled his saviours under.

Lauren he had lost. She had tried everything and the decision to end their relationship had come to her slowly. She prided herself on her loyalty and he knew that the failure of a marriage was, to her, the hallmark of a disappointed life. Becoming grandparents had established a fine thread between them that he understood should never be used to pull her closer. Though she had once cared for him more deeply than he deserved, with little to show for it, he had eventually seen in her sad brown eyes that she no longer held a place open for him in her heart. There was no hostility between them, just the recognition that Lauren had received a poor bargain and that Panenka owed her a debt of distance. Once Arthur started school, she sold their old house and moved further north to live on her own terms for the first time, more than twenty-five years later than planned. There remained echoes of her in his world as Marie-Thérèse was still close to her, though missed her, and Arthur often reported on his kind grandmother who lived in a house that he said was 'easy to draw.'

As he lay there, recovering from his headache and lost in night thoughts, the door swung on its hinges and the landing light cast an elongated trapezoid onto the floor. Arthur, who often entered his grandfather's bedroom in the way a sheriff might enter a saloon, paused in the doorway until he was sure Panenka was in there.

'Come on in and close the door quietly, Arthur – don't wake your mother.'

'Half way.'

'All right – half way. Let a bit of light in but not too much.'

Arthur pounded the few short steps across the room, and slid under the duvet at the foot of the bed, emerging at the pillow end to nestle backwards into Panenka's shoulders. Within a few deep breaths Arthur was already back to a safe sleep, and the night, so empty of answers, was again Panenka's alone.

# Chapter 7: Break Room

Marie-Thérèse sat in the changing room, scrolling through her phone. There was a limit to how long she could delay there – ostensibly getting her Tupperware salad box from her bag – before her absence would need explaining. She was required to take a half-hour break every six hours and had recently discovered that this was the hardest part of the day for someone struggling to get into character as a trainee manager. The break room upstairs was supposed to be shared between the floor staff and the managers, though it was only the junior managers who used it. Those with their own offices – who had a lunch *hour* – either ate at their desks or used the cafés nearby.

Out on the shop floor she could play her role but the break room, with its backstage informality, made her feel at her most fraudulent. Management was all about imposition: telling other grown-ups what to do; telling people she had gone for drinks with what to do; telling people she had complained to about Vincent what to do. It felt unnatural to her to have to redefine those relationships, outgrow them, shed them. It didn't seem like something a nice person would do.

She texted Carla:

> MT: How long can a person hide in the changing room before they start rumours?

She was surprised that Carla answered immediately.

> C: Depends on whether you're hiding alone. Who is he?

> MT: U not in work today?

C: Hungover. Told my boss I had a female issue. Bored. Can U go sick too?

MT: Can't. Am a grown-up now.

C: Is it OK to go online when you're sick?

MT: Best not to. We're told to check social media with sick notes. It's an easy catch.

C: Why U hiding?

MT: Nobody to sit with on my lunch break. I am a corporate monster.

C: FK that. Get them to bring U breakfast in bed. U R the boss now.

MT: Better go. Wanna meet later?

C: Best not. Gotta act sick.

MT: K. xx

When Marie-Thérèse arrived into the break room there were two men from the warehouse sitting at a four-seater table and two cashiers sitting diagonally from each other at another four-seater, taking up the whole space with their lunches and magazines. Marie-Thérèse stalled for a second, a second that was overlong in her own mind. Kathy, one of the cashiers, took the decision for her:

'Here, let's get this out of your way, Marie-Thérèse. Plonk your lunch down there.'

'You're fine – don't disturb yourself,' said Marie-Thérèse, trying to be nice but only complicating things.

'Look, it's no trouble.'

Marie-Thérèse took the seat she was offered, hyper-aware of how everything might come across to the others. She popped open the lid of her salad box, the same sort of lunch she had always brought in, but which now stood in vivid contrast to the chicken baguettes and crisps that the others were eating.

The men were engrossed in their phones and the tabloids. Marie-Thérèse hoped that their silence was innocent rather than calculated.

'Have you got any plans for the weekend?' she asked as naturally as she could, her hand across her mouth to avoid spitting salad shrapnel.

'It's only Wednesday – I haven't even thought about it,' said Kathy.

Marie-Thérèse realised she had asked the wrong stock question. She tried to rescue it. 'I know what you mean – maybe I plan these things too much.'

'You're right though – with family days out you have to think ahead. I'm always doing things at the last minute.'

The conversation stalled and rolled back down the hill towards her. The other cashier across from Kathy was Marian, or Marilyn or something, and had started a week or two earlier. Marie-Thérèse had interviewed her for the job and marked her down for being too uncommunicative, but she was overruled by her boss and she got hired based on her cash handling experience.

'How are you settling in?' Marie-Thérèse asked.

Marian or Marilyn, whose uniform was missing a name badge, was reading a cookery magazine and didn't respond.

'Marianne!' said Kathy. 'Marie-Thérèse was asking you something.'

'Oh sorry. I didn't hear you.'

'I was wondering how you're getting on. It's been a week or two now, hasn't it.'

'Fine thanks. Everyone's been really nice,' said Marianne, then awkwardly, 'Thanks for picking me for the job!'

'Oh, I wasn't checking up that way,' said Marie-Thérèse. 'I know it can be hard being new.'

'You're not fully broken-in until you've had your first night out with us,' said Kathy. 'Maybe answer that after Friday's drinks.'

It was the first work night out in ages that Marie-Thérèse hadn't been told about or invited to. She wondered whether her exclusion had been an oversight or a conscious decision – had she slipped off the grapevine or was it that people would relax more if she wasn't there?

'I'm not too crazy about this idea of Barvich coming in for Juilini,' said one of the men at the other table, having digested the article that had kept him quiet. 'He hasn't played regularly enough. The whole run-in has been about not messing with the team and formations and all that crap. All they need to do is keep it simple and don't blow it.'

'Juilini is a donkey,' said the other, summarily.

Seneca's run of form had gradually become more prominent in the break room conversation, as all shades of fan – casual or committed – started becoming more vocal with their punditry.

'If you look at the fixtures,' he continued, 'they could lose one of the last couple of games and still go up. But they're going to bottle it. They always get caught up in the drama and the pressure, then it gets inside their heads and they start thinking "Don't screw it up," and once that happens...' He gestured a bomb exploding over his lunch tray.

Marie-Thérèse focussed on her salad as the two women got back to their magazines. What if they mentioned Panenka? Did they even know that she was his daughter?

'But they can't keep having these near misses,' he resumed. 'It gets to the point where it must be purely psychological.'

'They're too fragile. Too much history,' said the other.

Marie-Thérèse was chewing self-consciously; a flush of red worked its way up her throat.

'Best be getting back,' he said, folding his newspaper. 'You ladies take your time.'

'What are you talking about?' said Kathy. 'You were up ten minutes before us. Not to mention your unofficial "comfort" breaks.'

'Now now, Kathy. Not in front of the management,' he said as he pushed his sandwich wrapper into a swing bin.

Marie-Thérèse smiled along with the banter, relieved to be included in it.

'Listen to them,' said Marianne when they had gone. 'My boyfriend is like that at the moment. He never used to come to the matches with us and now it's all, *Ssshhh, the game is on*.'

'Pure tribal,' said Kathy. 'Is your kid into it?'

'Not really,' said Marie-Thérèse. 'An hour and a half is a bit long for children.'

'My son's the same,' said Kathy. 'And there are too many matches – every weekday night there's something on TV. It's like a soap opera.' She lifted herself up from the table and took her tray over to the bin. 'We'd better go downstairs and stop that lot making a mess of the place.'

'I'll follow you down in a minute,' said Marie-Thérèse, pointing at her half full lunchbox.

She needed a moment to reset. Each day was about getting used to things, she thought, pushing her hair behind her ear and unconsciously rubbing the hidden alopecia patch.

On her way back downstairs, her boss asked her to drop into his office for a quick second. He was about the same age as Marie-Thérèse, which was normal in retail where you either went into management early or not at all. Though they had worked closely together for a while, she didn't know him that well. He had advised her that this was a people business, but only up to a point: it wasn't for those who needed to feel popular. At first, when he encouraged her to go for promotion, Marie-Thérèse was unsure how to interpret his interest in her career. When a manager at work praises and pays attention to you, it's natural to wonder about his motives. She had talked this through with Carla who, throughout her own spicy career, had found romance both up and down the organisation chart. Carla was a sage in her own way, and listened carefully to Marie-Thérèse's description of various one-to-one situations and moments of ambiguity. Her diagnosis was that the boss was probably not the type to use flattery for selfish reasons. The signal to watch out for, she said, was if he ever got *confessional*, especially about things not being rosy with his wife.

'This is nothing to worry about,' he began. 'I only wanted to check in and make sure you're getting the support you need.'

'Things are good, thanks. There's lots to learn, but like I said at the interview, I'm up for that.'

'Relax, you already have the job. It's a big change and everyone struggles a bit at the beginning. It's an adjustment. Anything you want to talk about from your side?' he asked, tapping his pen.

She didn't think there was any point in mentioning the alopecia. He would end up getting the wrong idea and smothering her with the corporate pastoral care programme: buddies, mentors and the like.

'In that case, there's one quick thing before we finish,' he said, opening what she recognised as her HR file. 'Your probation period is up soon and you're doing great, which means we'll need to think about which store to assign you to.'

'Oh. I hope you know I'm happy here,' she said, as casually as she could. 'I'm not necessarily looking for a move, but obviously—'

'Look, it's your choice. But sometimes, if you're appointed to the same store you were promoted from, there can be some complications. *Believe me*,' he said, leaning in and lowering his voice to a managerial I'm-on-your-side whisper, '*I know there are some difficult personalities here*.'

She nodded as though only an idiot would disagree, though inwardly he made her feel like she might be that idiot.

'Where else could I go... and when?'

'I can't make any promises but if you have a preference, let me know and I'll see what I can do. And if you decide to stay here, well then, I'd be lucky to have you,' he beamed, shutting the file and placing his hands on top of it.

Marie-Thérèse thanked him and left his office, feeling disoriented, as though a firework had gone off too close to her ear. She punched the button for the lift and ran through the conversation again in her head – it had been a flash meeting, designed to prevent her from raising any tectonic problems. She had been trained to do the same.

The thought of moving hadn't ever occurred to her – once Arthur got into the local school she had assumed that they would both stay. But in a way, if she wanted to she could choose to view this as the opening she was looking for. Starting over in situ had proved complicated, both at work and with Vincent. Maybe to move on she had to move away, like her mother had done. The past year since her separation had kept the prospect of change in her life simmering without bringing it to the boil – she hadn't yet done anything irreversible. The longer she left the split with Vincent unfinished, the greater the risk that their relationship would fuse together again, and though it was oversimplifying to say that she'd been too busy to end her marriage properly, they were certainly overdue a proper conversation about it.

And what about her dad? When she moved in with him it had been a bold statement. But directed at whom? It was a time when her mother had started to reclaim her own life, and when Marie-Thérèse had already fledged. But it was also the first big decision she had taken without the support of her mother, which meant that if it broke she would have to fix it alone. At the time she had said that she wanted Arthur to know his grandfather, and that had provided a temporary basis for things until she was able to admit that she missed her dad. She convinced everyone, including herself, that the past couldn't be mended with a watchmaker's curiosity about how it worked. It was better to choose a new starting point. And now here she was, considering the possibility of leaving him. Why was it that whenever she recalculated her relationships she was always left with these uncomfortable remainders?

She started but then deleted a text to Carla. Hearing voices chattering from within the lift, she decided to duck down the back stairs instead, and one step at a time, she gathered herself. The bright artificial light of the shop floor snapped her back to the here and now. She decided to do a walk-around to see how the shift was going; solve a selection of simpler problems. Word could have already leaked out that she could be leaving soon, which would only make things harder. The men from the break room were gathered around a pallet that should have been put away ages ago, so she went to see what they were doing. When she was first promoted she had been advised not to carry keys, as you never caught anyone doing anything if they could hear you coming.

# Chapter 8: Anthony

Anthony had been listening impatiently for several minutes as BABA numbered the points he was making to Teddy.

'First, travel does not broaden the mind. Being a tourist is a way of being the village idiot in a strange place for a few days. Who on earth would ask a tourist for their opinion about anything important? An imbecile, that's who.

'Second, travellers who return from their journeys don't enrich the lives of those around them. Ideas are not an import/export business. It might sound exotic to sketch out the principles of some foreign way of living, but that sort of passing fascination is no more than a holiday romance.

'Third—'

'Excuse me, I would like to speak after this point,' said Anthony.

'*Third* – and I will give way after this – the traveller arrives back infected, riddled with a condition that can't be cured by quarantine or any known antidote. It takes over body and mind—'

'Let me guess – is it long-windedness?' asked Anthony.

'Please don't interrupt my flow,' implored BABA. 'Over the course of completing two degrees, my mind has been trained into an orderly way of thinking—'

'It's more like one degree. After all, you have a pass degree and an honours degree in the same subject. One is simply a progression from the other – technically they're not *separate*,' said Anthony, making the point he tended to make most regularly and enjoyably.

'Don't vex me, Anthony. I won't be vexed!' insisted BABA. 'As I was saying, which condition is it that travellers acquire and which resists treatment?'

BABA was giving eye contact to each of his interlocutors in turn and willing them to complete his thought.

'I give in. Explain yourself, O wise one,' said Anthony.

'Restlessness!' revealed BABA. 'A person who travels is no sooner back and settled into their old routine than they are already mooning over pictures of their next destination. They are never mentally and physically in the same place for long. When they travel they are full of daydreams about their real life back home, and when at home they project how things would be so much better if they were in Santiago or Khartoum, or even a little B&B fifty miles down the road overlooking a bay. Humans are by nature romantic creatures. By that I don't mean full of love: I mean that they like the idea of things more than the reality of them. A traveller can't possibly understand the world, because most of the people *in* the world have no choices and no options. In other words, they are poor bastards, God help them. The traveller, however, can always leave. I see it with my students all the time.'

BABA was a teacher whose mission was to make native speakers of the hopeless cases he taught, mostly casual workers from the Crucible. It was a job that suited his training but not his temperament. He had a pedantic mind and it was difficult for him to stare out at indifferent faces every day and work spiritlessly through a curriculum that was heavily focussed on getting the students into low paid contracts. It included all the vocabulary a person might need in order to master the local bureaucracy or attain a customer service level of fluency. He was a lot older than his students and he could tell that, to them, he was a man of sexless, characterless middle age. In all the years he had been teaching – he called it lecturing – he had never been sent a postcard from a past pupil whose life he had changed, nor had he contributed to the crowded marketplace of the world's ideas. He was a man with one suit, which was really more of a dogtooth jacket with slacks, who taught the language with as little flair as possible. But BABA had just enough learning to make the other customers at Vincent's doubt themselves whenever they tried to pronounce a word they had only ever seen written down. It had been his habit to sit and read Montaigne on a bar stool, eavesdropping on the general discussion, and sipping a glass of crème de menthe, rarely having a second drink in an evening. His original declaration was that, as the sole crème de menthe drinker in Vincent's, he would leave once the whole bottle was finished and find himself another place and other company. That was merely one of the many ways in which BABA tried to make himself sound interesting to others, but he had overestimated the attention span of men who had little staying power for ultimatums that take a long time to ultimate. Vincent changed the bottle when it was empty and the whole business was forgotten about.

'You're overthinking things,' said Vincent. 'I remember when I was young, one of the neighbours slept with a girl who was hardly out of school, and a year or so later she calls over with a baby and leaves him with it.'

'What did he do?' asked Teddy, who was wondering whether he'd be allowed to have one of the medicinal-looking drinks that BABA was sipping.

'He raised the child,' said Vincent. 'He and his mother raised it – a lovely little baby girl, who had already been named. Claudine or Claudette it was. So he took all the overtime he could get, working on machines – heavy work. Ended up missing a thumb at the knuckle. Years later, when Claudine or Claudette was a bit older, he decides that he's going to have the adventures he never had and packs up and leaves the country.'

'Where did he go?' asked Anthony.

'Isle of Man,' said Vincent.

'Was he gay?' asked Teddy.

'He had a daughter for God's sake!' said Anthony. 'The Isle of Man is an island near Wales. They have cats with no tails and that sort of thing.

'What I'm saying is that sometimes travel can help a person make a fresh start,' explained Vincent.

'You can't run away from your troubles – they're all up here anyway,' said BABA tapping his temple.

'What about Panenka?' said Anthony, dropping his voice and swivelling his head, left then right. 'He could have gone off and played elsewhere, earned more money. Let the whole thing become a memory. But he didn't. He stayed, and look what happened.'

'Careful now,' said Vincent over his shoulder, climbing a stepladder behind the bar to dust the bottles. 'Anyone could walk in.'

'I know, and I'm not looking to discuss him in his absence, but there is some truth in what I'm saying,' said Anthony. The others avoided agreeing with him but didn't dispute his point either.

'Why – what happened?' asked Teddy, having decided that he was going to stick to beer.

'I think we had better change the subject,' said Vincent in a lowered voice from the top step. 'If you're curious about the past, Teddy, then that's what the internet is for.'

'I wasn't being nosey,' said Teddy. 'It's more that I meet him most days but don't know much about him. I don't even know what he works at.'

'He doesn't usually share those details with us,' said Anthony. 'That man has had countless jobs over the years: printing, machine calibration, all sorts of repairs and restorations. At one stage he asked me whether there were any jobs going at the delivery company where my wife works, or *worked,* but he had already let his truck driver's licence lapse. Any time I ask him how work is going he always says something vague. I think he likes to keep moving around; doesn't like people getting to know him too well.'

'He has us – why would he need anyone else?' said Vincent.

'I like hanging out with you lot,' said Teddy. 'I think you talk about interesting things. Most of my friends at home tend to sit over their drink and talk about whatever. Seneca or stuff like that.'

'You're young,' said Anthony. 'Believe me, once you have lived through the things we talk about, they stop becoming interesting.'

'No need to be bleak,' said BABA. 'Young Teddy has a point. A man should mix with people who are at different stages of life. That's what keeps you open minded. Either that or follow Montaigne: retire at thirty-eight and live out your days reading books and writing your ideas.'

'Please God tell us you're not writing a book, BABA,' said Anthony.

'I am not, but if I did it would have a troll called Anthony in it.'

'With that tribute, gentlemen,' said Anthony, 'I will say good night. BABA – you should use that green mouthwash you drink to rinse out the bitter words on your tongue.'

Anthony buttoned up his mac and left Vincent's. It was evidently the eve of bin day in the Crucible, and loose bits of plastic packaging were being blown out of overstuffed dumpsters and doing balletic turns down the street. Anthony had not had much to drink but his brain was tired from the working day and he couldn't settle on any one thing to think about on the short walk home. The house was just as he had left it a few hours before when he had cooked dinner for his wife and himself. He had waited quietly in the living room for any sound upstairs of her fork scraping or her cup being moved. There he sat in the dark with the TV off and with no sound but the rubbing together of his stockinged feet, unconsciously bestowing on each other the affection that was missing from his own life.

Before leaving for Vincent's, he had gone up to tell his wife that he was stepping out and would be back later, and to offer whatever it was she needed. The response, or non-response, had been the same for weeks now: the distant silence of a lighthouse far out at sea; an unreachable quiet.

Now returned, he let himself into the house, easing the lock open so that its stiff mechanism wouldn't disturb her if she were sleeping. The kettle was left plugged in from earlier on when he had decided against making a noisy cup of tea. Removing his shoes at the bottom of the staircase, he climbed it two steps at a time, using his internal mine detector to avoid the creaky boards, and trying not to spill the glass of water he had brought with him. There was a small bookcase on the landing where he kept short fiction, poetry, factual books, journals. A sort of insomniac's library, from which he selected an anthology he remembered as a comforting volume, but it was all wrong for his mood and out of season, the snowy images clashing with the humidity of the evening. He got changed into his pyjamas on the landing. As he opened the door barely wide enough for him to enter, he could see her sleeping on her right side with her back to him, her cropped brown hair looking tufty and duckling-like. He climbed into the bed carefully, pressing his tongue against his front teeth as he eased his weight onto the mattress, trying not to alter its topography in a way that she could feel. When all this had first started happening he would whisper goodnight or kiss the back of her ear, and once he had even spooned in beside her with his arm resting on hers. She made no response to these affections and, if anything, his intuition was that they were unwelcome and caused her distress. So Anthony had learned to lie by himself in the bed, beside the woman he had once made happy. Whatever had happened that day would sink to the bottom of his mind and his finishing thought would be how utterly unwanted he was.

# Chapter 9: Cesar Fontaine

The breakthrough in Panenka's football career came when the first team manager was sacked by Seneca, ostensibly for continuing poor form, but in reality as a way of covering up the insidious performance drug culture that he had brought to the club. In his place they appointed a man who had been out of work for eighteen months and who had never coached a top-tier team before. His name was Cesar Fontaine.

Cesar Fontaine had previously taken a small Northern side up two divisions in five years, a period during which they had also enjoyed a cup run as far as the quarter finals. He had achieved this with practically no budget, using his network of contacts and scouts in the lower divisions to find players who had been overlooked or who had otherwise failed to impress during the brief opportunities afforded them. What made him different was that he was in every respect a footballer's manager. He believed in spending time with his players, both on the training ground and afterwards in long trust-building conversations. His philosophy was that of a Jesuit, building players from the inside and instilling in them a spiritual love of football.

Seneca was broke, which meant Cesar had to build a team based on the non-existent youth ranks, by bringing in new recruits on free transfers, and by recalling Seneca players who had been loaned out to other clubs to cut wage costs. Among them was Panenka, who one Friday evening received a call from Cesar himself telling him he was to report to the training ground the following Monday. He was also asked to lay an extra place for dinner at his home that evening.

Cesar arrived at their flat carrying flowers for Lauren, a bouquet he said that he had picked himself from his own garden. He was wearing a long beige trench coat over a brown suit, with a red shirt and a black tie. He was whip-thin, with parenthetical lines either side of his mouth, and deep sad eyes. As Panenka waited nervously to meet his new boss, he stood listening to Lauren and Cesar chatting in the hall about the flowers, with an invitation extended for her to come visit Cesar's garden and take cuttings of anything she admired. Panenka would come to know Cesar Fontaine's manners as an intrinsic part of his philosophy, which was based on sincerity and consideration as the foundation for all human relationships. He made other people feel interesting. It was charisma.

The meal was a relaxed one, though Cesar spent hardly any time discussing football and directed most of his attention towards Lauren. He had a reputation for eccentricity and was knowledgeable about a broad range of subjects, though he was also happy picking up ordinary gossip or talking about TV. He liked to ask questions and reacted thoughtfully to what he heard, weighing the views of others without judging them. The closure of the town's run-down swimming baths had grieved him greatly, and he sought Lauren's opinion on his plans for Seneca to take it over as a community project. When he was leaving, he requested a few minutes alone with Panenka.

'My friend, I am going to change things and I'm interested in those who are loyal and committed to me and to Seneca. I know you've grown up with this club, but in terms of personal loyalty, that's a relationship you and I will have to build together. I need to respect you as a man. The way you conduct yourself on the pitch, with your team mates, with your wife, the way you carry yourself as you walk down the street, and your ability to confront your own limitations, these are all things I'll watch in order to find out who you are. You'll go through a lot with me, but it will be for your own good as a person and as a player. If you're not ready for that, I'll facilitate a free transfer. I say that without menace. I want you to succeed in your career, but Seneca will be a different club from now on. When you show up to training on Monday there'll be a lot of new players there, and many others will have left. I'm looking for leaders: players who'll get on the ball. I want men who will provide an example to the town and who will show the young players that the most meaningful talent is a capacity for hard work. You're about half a stone overweight, so we'll start there. Do you understand me?'

Panenka accepted the proposition. Cesar patted him on both shoulders and left, climbing into a beautifully polished Alfa without turning around to say goodbye.

That night in bed he and Lauren discussed Cesar, with Panenka playfully accusing her of flirting. She would only concede that good manners are never wasted and that Cesar was the first football person she had met whom she felt like trusting. It wasn't his charm that got through to her – which any salesman could fake – but the fact that his coat so clearly had a torn pocket that he didn't hide. The main thing, she said, changing the subject and pulling Panenka towards her, was that he wouldn't be on loan any more, so she would have him at home and all to her herself more often.

During the first half of the first season together, everyone assumed that Cesar Fontaine was going to be sacked. The clear-out had been brutal. The wisdom in the press was that Cesar had the right idea but had brought about too much change at once. While the young players were developing technically, the poor form was damaging their confidence and they were playing in a nervous, inhibited way. Panenka was among those who were struggling and, while he responded well to Cesar's man-management, which he found inspirational on a personal level, he needed more guidance. It was fine being told to express himself and play the game he was afraid to play, but their marking on set pieces was disorganised, and they got murdered on counter-attacks. After a couple of heavy defeats at home, including against rivals Olympik, the mood became sombre at the training ground. As they sat around in a horseshoe having one of the general football-loving conversations that the players had started to grow tired of, Panenka put his hand up and asked that they discuss the pressure.

'Go on,' said Cesar Fontaine.

'We need more instruction. You keep asking me to do vaguely inventive things, and I don't have the time on the ball to do that if we're constantly in chaos. Don't get me wrong, I see your vision and I'm up for it, but maybe we're not as good as you think we are.'

'Do you all agree about this?' asked Cesar, in response to which there was an apologetic murmuring of confirmation. 'Right: stand up.'

They braced themselves for some sort of recrimination, but Cesar simply organised them into groups of fours and fives and began running through what he saw as basic drills, though many of the younger players, including Panenka, had never done them before. After that, Cesar simplified the training regime and got the team to work to more predictable playing patterns. He acknowledged that he was learning too. His previous experience had been in integrating young players into a more settled team, and he had not factored in that a team built entirely on inexperienced enthusiasm would need a different type of preparation.

They lost their next game, but they had played well enough to buy Cesar a little time. After Christmas, their results stabilised, and though they had ended the season one place above the relegation zone, the fans were encouraged by the strong finish, and Cesar kept his job.

Towards the end of that season, Panenka took his first ever penalty as a professional player. The penalties had always been taken by strikers up to that point, but Panenka had been playing well and had dribbled – albeit clumsily – into the box to draw the foul. They were already ahead and he saw it as a low-pressure kick. Though he hadn't practised his penalties he knew that he would drill it high to the keeper's left, which would be his natural side as a left-footer. He took a short run up and cracked the ball against the crossbar.

Seneca won the game ultimately, but the penalty miss led to some nerves in the second half and affected Panenka's rhythm for the remainder of the game. Afterwards, Cesar took him aside and said 'In my opinion, it's always so much more beautiful and dramatic to hit the woodwork.'

# Chapter 10: Playground

Once they reached the playground entrance Arthur abandoned his scooter and ran towards the climbing frame, leaving Marie-Thérèse and Panenka to drink their coffees on a graffitoed bench, sitting on the bad word that was sprayed across it. The playground itself reflected the Crucible's general state of disrepair: the broken stuff looked like it had been broken a long time, and the whole thing was nearing the point where it could soon cease to be a place for families and instead become a meeting point of notoriety for teenagers.

'Ow, that's hot. What do they make this coffee with – plutonium?' said Panenka, wincing as he sipped through the hole in the lid.

'I think they overheat bad coffee,' said Marie-Thérèse. 'I knew not to expect much when the van had ice cream decals on it.'

Arthur was already over at the monkey bars, hanging upside down by his knees and chatting to another boy.

'Is that someone from Arthur's class?' asked Panenka.

'No, but he's good at picking up other children. He's social that way.'

'Is he safe hanging like that – won't he get dizzy?'

'He'll be fine. He has your natural athleticism.'

'So that's where it went.'

'You're doing all right. At least you look better than *him,*' said Marie-Thérèse about one of the older dads. 'Long hair. It never turns the clock back. I bet he's always had that look. Why do men find one hairstyle and then mate with it for life?'

'I never thought about it.'

'Although you're getting a little fluffy yourself, now that I notice. Time to visit Donnie's for a trim.'

'I know, I know. Donnie's has been closed for a few weeks, so I've been putting it off. Anthony told me Donnie sliced his hand on a can of peaches – severed a nerve.'

'Is he okay?'

'That's all I know. Typical Anthony: at most he tells you half a story. But I promise I'll get it sorted. I don't want to embarrass you.'

They watched the dad playing some sort of toy badminton with his son and over-instructing him.

'I don't think this place has been renovated since I used to come here,' said Marie-Thérèse. 'The swings were missing seats even back then. I bet I could find Carla's name on a bench here, along with the names of the guys she went out with. A few benches, probably.'

Panenka, who had no recollection of that period of her life, said nothing.

The playground was quiet by playground standards: a few couples with toddlers who were too young to go on anything, and some dog people talking about dog stuff and carrying their little bags of shit.

'I heard you up and about again last night,' said Marie-Thérèse, trying to refit her leaking coffee lid. 'It's becoming a regular thing now.'

'It comes and goes,' said Panenka without looking at her.

'Is that it?'

Panenka hesitated. He wasn't yet ready to say more. Marie-Thérèse let it go.

Arthur came running towards them with flushed cheeks.

'I need a drink,' he said. 'We're making a base in the sand.'

'Here you go,' said Marie-Thérèse handing him a water bottle from her bag. He slugged it down before dashing back to a group of boys digging a hole in what used to be a sand pit, but which was now more of a dirt pit.

'Look, Dad, I wanted to talk to you about something,' started Marie-Thérèse. 'There are some changes ahead.' She had to stop herself using the management tricks for breaking bad news. 'They're going to confirm my promotion in work.'

'I'm delighted for you. Congratulations.'

'Thing is, part of the deal is that I get the chance to work at a different store. I mean, I haven't made a decision yet, but there are all sorts of reasons why that might make sense. A fresh start at work, and, well, with everything else.'

The shuttlecock landed near Panenka and he threw it back to the long-haired dad, who didn't say thanks.

'It's possible that I'll be moving out, Dad. Arthur and me. Both of us.'

Panenka stared across to where Arthur was playing, without reacting.

'Look, I haven't decided finally and there are a lot of details to figure out,' she continued, 'so it wouldn't happen for a while, but it's only fair that I tell you ahead of time.'

'Where will you go... where will you be? Have you spoken to your mother about this?' he asked.

'We talked last night about it. You can probably guess what her advice is. There's a job going in one of the stores up that way too. Rent might be cheaper than here, which is important if I'm going to be paying it alone.'

'But that's miles away. What will you do about schools and Vincent and everything?'

'You're going to have to not talk me out of this, Dad.'

They could see Arthur sitting down in a pit he had dug with two other boys, assessing its depth. The sand would be all over the house later.

'I'll do whatever I can to help, you know that,' said Panenka.

'I don't want you to think I'm leaving you behind – that Arthur and I don't want you in our lives.'

'I would never think that,' he said softly.

Arthur came over carrying a squashed football he'd found.

‘I think I’m tired. And hungry,’ he said, his fringe slicked and sweaty.

‘Here, show me that football,’ said Marie-Thérèse. ‘We can’t bring that home. The boy who owns it would be upset.’

‘It’s bursted anyhow,’ said Arthur, tossing it away.

‘*Burst.* C’mon – say goodbye to the boys you were playing with.’

Arthur waved goodbye behind him without even looking.

‘We’ll talk about it later okay?’ said Marie-Thérèse in an aside to Panenka.

‘Talk about what?’ interrupted Arthur.

‘Your mother wants me to grow my hair long,’ answered Panenka, taking his hand.

Marie-Thérèse drove while Arthur played with her phone in the back seat. Unable to discuss the one thing worth talking about, she and Panenka said little, each processing and aware of the other’s processing. Panenka could sense Marie-Thérèse and Arthur just inches away from him; their easy proximity felt extravagant, given how scarce it would soon become. If only there was a way of storing and rationing it so that he need never have to miss them. Habituated loneliness was bearable, but the heart was not built to endure glimpses of what it could never truly have.

His mind became a parliament of factions. Noble thoughts about putting Marie-Thérèse and Arthur first felt right but untrue, as a more honest, but selfish, counterpoint wished things otherwise. It had always been this way for him. While he struggled to understand which of the voices among that internal cacophony was his own, he knew that from the outside he would seem a brooding, disconnected man. Words always took too long to find, and in the meantime the silence conspired against him and separated everything.

# Chapter 11: BA

When Panenka arrived at Vincent's later that evening, it was as if his own mood had preceded him. There was a lingering atmosphere of tension, as an earlier conversation between Anthony and BABA had misfired and the usual banter, which so often provided the flint for a conversational spark, had tipped into more personal criticism, leaving both men guarded as if on their stools between rounds.

As proprietor, it fell to Vincent to lift the mood.

'I had a customer in this morning, and he tells me he's in the cigar business,' he started. 'So he went out to his car to get some samples, while I made small talk with the wife. She answers me in this tiny little whisper, so low that I couldn't hear her unless I ducked my head in really close. I thought she might have had laryngitis or a strep throat or something, and I didn't want her to strain herself, so I pretended like I heard what she was saying. Then, when we were in the back discussing the order, he explained to me that his wife has lost her voice for good – want to know how?'

'Why not,' said Anthony with begrudging interest.

'She was making a costume for her daughter, who was supposed to be an angel in a school play or something, so the pocket of her apron was full of offcuts of cloth. She was smoking while she worked and a piece of hot ash fell into her pocket and the material went whoosh! into flames.' Vincent used his hands to show what a whoosh looked like. 'It burned the skin across her tummy and private area. She screamed so much and so loudly that she burst her larynx and lost her voice permanently.'

The others, who had been desperate for something to cheer them up, withdrew into their vivid imaginations.

'What kind of man confesses a thing like that about his poor wife?' said Anthony. 'That kind of detail shouldn't be shared.'

'It's the way some people are' said Teddy. 'They can't help wanting others to know what their life is like.

'When you run a café-bar you get used to people saying strange things,' said Vincent. 'An office type was in the other day and in the middle of his coffee, he gets up and asks me what's wrong with my wife. I was about to throw him out when I realised he was asking about my *Wi-Fi*.'

'What about you, Teddy?' asked Anthony. 'You're young and new and carefree – you must have some bit of sunshine you can bring into the conversation.'

Teddy was sitting with a glass of red wine, which he had self-consciously ordered though he was now regretting it. He was thirsty from steaming the pots and would have preferred a cold beer.

'I was thinking of getting a tattoo done,' he said.

'What type?' asked Vincent

'Or more importantly, where?' asked Anthony.

'A few of my friends have tattoos – a lot of them are getting the names of their kids done,' said Teddy.

'It's probably so the mothers can tell which one is the father,' said Anthony.

'Children having children – it's crazy,' muttered BABA without looking up.

'I was only a few of years older than Teddy when we had Marie-Thérèse,' said Panenka. 'When you're young you don't realise how young you are.'

'You'd want to be careful if you're looking for work, though,' said Vincent, providing the employer's perspective. 'People might think you're the aggressive type if you have tattoos.'

'Actually,' said BABA, over his shoulder, 'in nature, distinctive markings are used to deter conflict, not initiate it. It wouldn't surprise me if most people who get tattoos turn out to be gentle souls who project a tough image as a way of avoiding trouble.'

'What design are you going to pick?' asked Panenka, who had Marie-Thérèse's name on his bicep.

'I was thinking I'd get something to do with Seneca,' answered Teddy. 'The crest or something. I think it's a safer bet than the name of a girlfriend—'

'Or even a wife!' interrupted Anthony.

'Yeah, or even a wife,' agreed Teddy. 'I mean, what if it doesn't work out? It's bad enough breaking up without having to get her face lasered off your arm. I was thi—'

'You don't need a tattoo for a woman to leave a permanent mark on you, believe me,' said Anthony. 'People who make a big show of their relationships are usually those who are insecure about them. Love is like getting lost in the woods. Shouting aloud that you're safe might make you feel better, but it doesn't mean you're not lost. If I can give you one piece of advice, my young dishwashing protégé—'

'My God,' started BABA. 'Is there no end to your bleak evangelism, Anthony?'

'Careful BABA. I don't want to make you cry again,' said Anthony.

'Oh please. You sit there with your face like a stopped clock, imparting your venom to the rest of us. You patronise Teddy who, unlike you, is not poisoned by cynicism. And you're always trying to drag others down – repeatedly belittling my academic record, for example. I don't expect special treatment: merely recognition of what I achieved through my own hard work.'

'From now on,' said Anthony with an ironic appeal to those around him, 'I am no longer playing along with this charade. As of this day, I am calling you BA, not BABA. One degree, one qualification.'

'Do NOT vex me Anthony!' said BABA firmly. 'I will not be vexed!'

'Take it easy you two,' said Panenka. 'This is getting personal.'

'Panenka, you should listen to what I am saying,' said BABA. 'He talks about you, too, when you're not here.'

'I do not! You're a shameless liar!' said Anthony, getting exercised.

'How dare you!' snapped BABA, 'You sat here the other evening, speculating about Panenka's personal matters and giving advice about what he should have done. All behind his back, like a little grass snake.'

'A lie! Panenka, this is all lies. BAB—, or should I say *BA* has no standards. He sits there with his big book, pretending to read it, but when it comes to real life, all that *supposed* learning, or lack of it, is revealed. A cheap troublemaker, that's all you are BA! Did you hear that, BA!'

'That's it!' said BABA standing up angrily. 'As I have said before, there are other places I can go. I'm a civilising influence on this place, but it's clear that some of you are beyond help. It's the way you were brought up.'

'BABA, sit down, don't be ridiculous,' said Panenka wearily. 'Let's all stay calm and take a breath.'

'I'm serious,' said BABA. 'Unlike you Anthony, I don't stay in relationships where I am clearly not wanted. I'll leave you to your self-pity. Vincent, before I go, I will give you one piece of advice that Montaigne would give if he were here: buy the damn TV.'

With that, BABA grabbed his book, swiped his dogtooth jacket from the back of the stool and marched out.

In his wake a low cloud of misery sat in the room. Had there been any other customers in that night, the incident would have been bad for business. It was just one of those days, of which there are a few in every calendar, that is only improved by being ended.

The silence was eventually broken by Teddy:

'Oh look,' he said. 'He left his glasses behind.'

# Chapter 12: Haircut

Panenka faced the next morning with a foggy tiredness. He perched on the edge of the bed with interlocked prayerful fingers, his mind lost in wordless thoughts. It had been a traumatic night on the bathroom floor with the Iron Mask, where he had done everything to suppress the groans that he longed to let ring throughout the house. The pain had eventually ebbed and he clambered back aboard his bed as if it were a raft, grabbing its sides and lying on his stomach, adrift on his own Crusoe-like despair.

Marie-Thérèse and Arthur had let him sleep through breakfast and by the time he arrived downstairs they had already left. The empty kitchen was in disorder from the morning rush that had taken place without him. Standing by the sink was a small porridge pot left soaking and there was a basket of dirty laundry abandoned in front of the open washing machine. Panenka sorted through it and found socks rolled-up, tracksuit bottoms with pants still inside them, pockets with tissues, and t-shirts that had sauces smeared around the neckline.

The water was already cool by the time he showered, rubbing the soap around his softening body. His weight had stayed stable during his forties, but he could see that his body shape had changed and grown a little thicker around the middle, each passing year adding another tree ring. The cleft in his chin – which Marie-Thérèse used to kiss, back in the old days – was losing its definition. Panenka often thought about what his doctor had said about keeping a little bit of weight for safety in case of illness, though the doctor himself was thin as a jockey.

He dried his hair, which he wore as he had always worn it: a practical footballer's cut, short all round with a side parting and tidy fringe, which, when it fell onto his forehead, as it did now, told him it was time for a trim. At Donnie's nobody was ever asked what style they wanted: they simply got a shorter version of what they already had. Donnie had learned to cut hair in the army and viewed barbering as something akin to getting your toenails cut or brushing your teeth. It was a maintenance job, and not something to develop ideas about.

He left for work with plenty of time to spare ahead of his midday shift and walked through the Crucible, slaloming between the crowds with his usual practised invisibility. The town authorities had recently given permission for a street market, though had done sweet nothing to support it. Traders were selling everything from watches to branded jeans to mobile phones, laid out on foldable tables or spilling from old vans. No permanent structures allowed, by order of a council with trust issues. Panenka had seen this type of initiative before. The council would let it run for a while as way of flushing out the black market, before shutting it down and confiscating everyone's goods. The traders knew what was going on but would take their chances for as long as it lasted.

Across town, he took a shortcut to the cathedral quarter where the streets were lined with single-door shops offering things like baking, flowers, shoe repairs, dry cleaning, hair extensions. Small-time, subsistence entrepreneurship. He stalled outside a barbershop, wavering over whether he had time for the haircut he had promised Marie-Thérèse and feeling conflicted about going somewhere other than Donnie's. As he stood there in his indecision, an elderly woman approached him slowly on the narrow, uneven path. She was smoking a cigarillo and exhaled lazily from the side of her mouth, her expression conveying the general impression that she was too old to give a damn. Her look was moneyed and eccentric, and she was walking a ratter on an extendable lead. Though it was warm, she wore a nicotine-yellow fake fur coat and a red beret with a white bobble, like a pimple. She made no concession to him as he stood sideways to let her pass, but he didn't take offence, momentarily hypnotised by that weird charisma unique people have. Panenka watched her disappear around the elbow in the road, taking her colour with her like a departing parade and leaving him alone again with the morning melancholy. The street was less alive without her. It struck him how unreliable age was as a measure of anything. All it did was count the distance from the start, when what truly mattered was the time remaining. Here he was, in mid-life, facing the Iron Mask, beyond which lay no future versions of himself; no eighty-something Panenka in fake fur. The street signs with bicycles locked to them would outlive him. So too would the dented 4x4 badly parked, as would the woman herself, even her scrawny dog. The world's bits and pieces, its props, its particularity; everything unimportant would outlast him. What was he but a vantage point? A retreating observer of all that would fill the moments in time that stretched out beyond him.

Through the barbershop window he could see men sitting and reading tabloids. There was nothing more than boredom going on, but to Panenka it looked almost spiritual, like a nativity scene. Life of any sort seemed profound once you considered what lay, or didn't lie, beyond it. He was drawn in and sat among them as people of significance, as participants in what he was going through: a father with his young son, whose curly hair had exploded; an office worker with his photo on a lanyard; two teenage boys playing on their phones, hardly talking; a workman of sorts, who had paint or plaster on his hands and whose trousers were a riot of zips and buckles. Central to it all was the barber, whom he watched in the mirror as she worked. About fortyish and dressed in black, like a backing singer, she wore a silver necklace with a precious stone that he didn't know the name of – the amber one. He envied her diligence and easy sense of purpose, her comfort in her own setting, like a cook chopping ingredients or a musician practising an instrument. It was life as it was supposed to be, so simple when observed from a distance.

He sat there with his thumbs pressing into each other, the world on the other side of the barbershop glass. Throughout his body, a flutter of panic was gathering. When his turn came he gestured to let someone else go ahead of him. His breathing was shallow and jumpy. Again he let his turn lapse, and then again, and again. The hour for the start of his shift came and passed, and yet still he sat there, inert in his sadness.

In time, the shop emptied.

'So,' she asked with a bright smile, 'what would you like?'

Panenka removed his hat and tracksuit top and took his place in the chair, which sighed under his weight.

'Take a little bit off,' he said. 'Please.' His voice was quieter than he had intended

She tied the black cape around him and adjusted the height of the chair with the foot pedal.

'You're not in too much of a hurry today then?' she asked. 'I think your hair looks a little longer than when you first came in.'

'I decided to take the day off.'

'Well, thanks for spending it with us,' she said. 'First time here?'

'I usually go to Donnie's – do you know it?'

'I haven't had the pleasure. I go to a salon myself.'

Working slowly, and with greater care than Donnie ever took, she manipulated his head gently to give herself a better angle, tilting his chin upwards and looking at his fringe from below. Panenka held himself just as she had placed him. It felt calming to sit there, passive and posable. He could feel her breath on his throat as she worked with calm concentration. It had been quite some time since anyone had treated him with such attention. A tide of vulnerability swelled within him.

'You've nice hair,' she said. 'Really fine, though. And you've kept your colour, which is unusual. Dark hair like yours usually goes badgery – you must have youthful genes.'

She brought her face close and folded his ear gently, her fingers cool against his skin. Tears brimmed at his lower lids. She was humming something, though not what was on the radio. The tips of her fingernails pressed intimately onto the back of his ear and Panenka was undone by the delicacy of it all. His eyelids shuttered down, and two fugitive tears escaped.

It took her a minute to notice.

'Oh my God! Did I cut you?' she said urgently, putting down her scissors.

Panenka shook his head, too overcome for the moment to speak.

'Are you all right? Here, let me take this off.' She whisked away the cape without letting the clippings fall onto his clothes. Underneath, his hands had been gripping the arms of the chair. She helped him up and brought him through to a back room where there was a small desk with paperwork and a kettle on it.

'Here, let me make you something.' She started looking around in the cupboard to see what she had. 'I don't usually keep too much temptation around – here, try one of these.'

Panenka sobered up to his embarrassment and accepted a shortbread biscuit as she made him a mug of tea.

'I'm sorry,' he eventually mumbled through a mouthful of crumbs. 'I don't know what that was about.'

'Is there someone I can call for you?'

'I'm fine. This never happens.'

He drank his tea self-consciously as she sat in his peripheral vision. He looked everywhere but at her. The radio in the barbershop, oblivious to everything, leaked all over the quiet between them.

'Here, let me pay for the haircut,' he said after a few slow minutes, reaching into his wallet. 'What do I owe you?'

'Oh, never mind that.'

'Seriously, let me pay. Please, I'd prefer to,' he said, and left too much money on the table.

She reached over and touched his wrist. 'Look,' she said, 'it's none of my business but… I know what it's like.'

He turned towards her.

'I mean, I know what it's like not to be okay.' Having said it, she withdrew her hand.

Panenka, hesitating at first, said nothing.

He thanked her for the unfinished tea and walked back into the barbershop to retrieve his tracksuit top. She followed him and he could sense her searching for eye contact, but it was too late.

He had already returned to himself.

He had already closed.

# Chapter 13: Olympik

In Cesar Fontaine's last season in charge of Seneca there was a falling-apart feeling about everything: the team, the club, the man. He had spent over six years in charge, during which time he had earned the fidelity and respect of the fickle Seneca fans, who were known for being loyal right up to the point when they weren't. But now, his crumpled trench coat and deep sad eyes had come to personify the worry that haunted the stadium. There was no single moment during the season that could be circled on the calendar as the start of the decline, but over a pattern of Saturdays, Seneca's 15,000 fans had come to the collective realisation that they had seen, and seen through, all of Cesar's tricks. Despite their love for the man, he was taking their team down. What he had performed for such a small club was indeed miraculous, but Cesar's thinking was now too readable, and other coaches found it all too easy to break down the naïve tactics that he persisted with. His erratic body language on the touchline was that of a man who had disappeared too far into his own self-doubt to think clearly.

Panenka tried to be a support to his coach during that time and invited him to dinner at their new house. Cesar had always been close to Lauren and in his easy charm with Marie-Thérèse, who was now aged three, they could still see glimpses of the great man whose gifts were so clearly slipping away. His usual fluency on subjects of all kinds was contracting into a narrow cycle of repetitive thoughts as he attempted to solve the problem of that cursed season by going over and over his strategy obsessively, as though trying to find the one blown bulb in a string of Christmas lights. As he was leaving, Lauren, whose loyalty and love were indistinguishable, spoke to him at his car, out of Panenka's earshot, offering words of hope and support probably, to a man left orphaned by his solitary greatness. She sank into Panenka's arms afterwards, full of the grief that is woken inside us from seeing those we care about suffer.

Before the season had started, Seneca fans had run their fingers down the fixture list in what they had expected to be a difficult year and, on seeing that their final game would be at home against Olympik, had been imploring the Gods to ensure that they would already be safe by then. It had been the game they had talked about most all season, and for a time it seemed like it would be irrelevant, as Seneca had looked condemned for much of the year. But their form during March and April had been good enough to make the last game meaningful in the most dangerous way possible.

While sporting drama is understandably recorded in history as a portrait of victories, the true experience of suffering football fans is that there is no more epic occasion than the last game of the season. It is a day when narrative arcs crash into each other; when talent and ability give way to mental fortitude; when teams competing for trophies come undone by those facing failure; when players with nothing to play for find the motivation to deny with relish another club's small share in that season's success; and it is when the impossibilities of arithmetic are definitively reckoned. On that final day of Cesar Fontaine's season it was clear that a draw or better for Seneca would ensure their survival and, more importantly, deny their rivals Olympik the league title. Anything less and Seneca would be relegated.

On the night before the match, Panenka was in bed beside Lauren, her cheek on his rounded shoulder, Marie-Thérèse asleep in the room next door. Back in those days he wore a little crucifix around his neck, a gift Lauren, an atheist, had given him years before. He liked to kiss it whenever he scored, a little affectation that he thought looked good in front of the home crowd. Lauren played with it absent-mindedly until he squeezed her fingers lightly and said 'don't.' So they lay there quietly, preoccupied, until she eventually drifted off and he spent another hour or more feeling the focus overcome his body, checking that the pure, dead concentration was ready, the little pulses of adrenalin released into his system as he did so. And as he checked his body – relaxed and fit and ready – he thought again about Lauren playing with the crucifix. There was always this flash of awareness just before he spoke to her, a moment when he knew what he was about to do and could avert it, but nevertheless made a conscious decision to withhold from her; to choose distance over intimacy. Why did he do that? He was never sure. It was a failure of spirit that would send her to sleep doubting herself and finding fault in her own faultless actions. All in order to satisfy some animal darkness of his. As he lay there, checking his body's state of preparation, he allowed himself a moment to wonder about these things.

On the morning of the match Panenka stuck to his diet sheet and his usual routine. They arrived at the stadium early for a massage and to prepare as a team. There were no interviews apart from those given by Cesar in which he was focussed and articulate. In the warm-up, the team looked ready. The younger players understood instinctively that in football, it's not possible to gain experience gradually. Those who, like Panenka, had been around a little longer, recognised the familiar adjustment in the body's chemistry: the heightened sensory awareness and the temporary sobriety in the emotions that would take their own course once the first sweat was broken.

Before the game, Cesar had spoken to each player quietly and separately to remind them first, of the most important thing they must do, then secondly, the thing they must not do. Cesar chose his words carefully. He reminded them about the dangers of adrenalin dump: that if they were seduced by the surge of cheap energy they would find themselves physically and mentally spent after twenty minutes. Cesar also put his philosophy to good use. He had often said that survival depended on finding a place within themselves where resided both the genius of sublime calm and the ability to play joyfully in the face of the most dehumanising pressure. He said that fear came from denial. They were afraid to lose and get relegated so they had talked away that possibility; lied to themselves about its existence. This was a mistake. To vanquish fear, and vanquish was the word he had used, he said you must look at each of the possibilities squarely and accept that it exists. It is the player who goes beyond his fear and beyond himself who will unlock this game, he said. The losing team would be the one that thinks of the latent mistakes that lie littered about the pitch.

Before Seneca had the chance to find their rhythm, it was already clear to Panenka that they wouldn't have the pace to match Olympik. They would need to tap a larger portion of the day's luck than they deserved. Within the first half an hour Olympik were already two goals up, and from the pitch he could hear the visiting fans already celebrating the glorious possibility of securing the first league title of their lifetime. Panenka had struggled. He was overrun in midfield and couldn't find time on the ball. Olympik had obviously done their preparation and knew that he liked to drop off to collect passes, so they man-marked him. But Seneca got an undeserved break: a ball floated in from a speculative free kick was spilled by the Olympik goalkeeper and poked in from close range. They deserved to be finished but instead found themselves galvanised as they went back down the tunnel at half time.

In the dressing room, Cesar was relaxed and clear thinking. He explained to them what had happened and how he was making a change in midfield to fix it. Panenka was asked to push on a little and given cover for doing so. It worked, and in the first ten minutes of the second half Panenka saw more of the ball and was able to set the pace a little. Olympik looked less certain of themselves when they were chasing the game. Panenka had become more confident, his passes were landing, he had options whenever he looked up, and his legs and lungs felt like they could go on forever.

It was a simple incident. Panenka was at the edge of the box and noticed the defender had hunched unusually low in front of him, inviting Panenka to pass him. As the player stooped, he moved his arms out wider than he should have in order to direct his teammate. Panenka put his toe under the ball and scooped it against the outstretched arm. The penalty was contrived and outrageous, but it was given. The referee was surrounded by Olympik players and was forced to back-pedal, drawing out his yellow card which he flashed at one player and then another, though it did little to deter their protests. It took several minutes for the chaos to subside, during which Panenka was pushed and elbowed, but he walked away with his hands held aloft in innocence. The Olympik players called him a cheat and a coward and other names that are used on football pitches to the shame of the players' mothers.

Panenka placed the ball himself. He was not the regular penalty taker but the situation was of his making, and Cesar affirmed that prerogative with a simple wave of his index finger. The penalty spot was chewed up as the Olympik players had dragged their studs across it during the dispute with the referee, but Panenka took his time and settled the ball down until he was happy that it wouldn't move. He checked that the ground was firm either side of the spot, to make sure his standing foot would be secure. The referee indulged this attention to detail, disregarding the complaints of the Olympik players, and the attempts by their goalkeeper to psych Panenka out by clanging his studs against the post.

Panenka stood outside the D of the box, signalling a lengthy run and a decision to go for power. Waiting for the referee, he made a conscious gesture to reach for and kiss his crucifix. Between the whistle and the start of the run there was a half-moment when he indulged a sweet surge of certainty as he briefly gave the eyes to shoot to his natural side. His run peaked just right, as he dinked his toe under the centre of the ball and made perfect contact to chip in a balletic arc towards the centre of the goal at chest height.

But Olympik's goalkeeper, uncharacteristically, had not moved early.

The ball floated meekly into his chest.

There were no more goals. Seneca were relegated and spent the next twenty-five years outside the top division. Olympik had won their first league title in living memory, at the ground of their bitterest rivals.

# Chapter 14: The Aftermath

When Panenka awoke the morning after the penalty miss, there was that briefest of moments before the full realisation again avalanched into his thoughts and he re-registered the impossibility of undoing his mistake. Lauren was already awake beside him, her eyes puffy and raw, her lips dry and parted but unready to speak. She reached out to stroke his shoulder.

After he had missed, and after the initial chorus of gasps had subsided, the stadium started to fill with a burbling of chatter. It continued and built up into a swarm of noise that remained unbroken during the futile push by Seneca in the closing minutes to salvage the game and their season. The manner of the penalty miss had astonished the crowd as if by bearing witness to it they had become accomplices. The hubris of it, the inappropriateness of it, the vanity of it, the betrayal of it. Yes, the betrayal of it. Of all the possible words, it was betrayal that those thousands of fans, in one wildfire of judgement, had settled upon to describe what they were suffering. They began purging the unwanted energy that coursed around the ground in an emetic response to the Panenka miss; a violent rejection of what had been done in their name, a blatant perversion of their collective will.

Is there any way to capture accurately the sound that Panenka heard that afternoon when the whistle definitively locked in the consequences of his actions for all time? It was a bellowing cacophony of aggression, which, as he crouched alone in the centre circle, left him like a small fishing boat among rolling, cliff-face waves. The stewards hurried him off the pitch, the swell of violence building all around him. For his own safety he was taken to the referee's changing room rather than Seneca's; his team-mates had blanked him at the end of the match. He sat there on the bench with his elbows on his thighs, the crucifix dangling below him. At first he tried to snap it off but the chain was too strong, so he lifted it over his head and threw it into the metal bucket in the corner. There was shouting in the corridor, voices telling other voices to calm down, followed by muted cheering from the Olympik players who had collected their trophy but had also picked up something dangerous in the air, more powerful than their triumphalism. Panenka sat for a long time in the stunned catatonia of the moment. His trance was broken by Cesar Fontaine, who came into the room quietly and sat beside him, pulling him into his shoulder as they both cried from their souls. 'My son, I'm so, so sorry,' was all he could say, kissing the top of Panenka's head and stroking his hair. 'My son, I'm so, so sorry.'

At home that evening, when the club had finally figured out how to escort him away safely, Lauren was sitting on the couch with Marie-Thérèse, who had been allowed to miss her bedtime and whose hair was still wet from her bath and smelled of coconut. Lauren jumped up and melted into Panenka's arms. Marie-Thérèse was grabbing his trouser leg to bring him over to the Lego house they had built, but his face was buried in his wife's collar bone, sobbing like a child himself. He swept his young daughter up onto his hip and they embraced as a family. Their lives, and his name, changed forever.

In the days that followed, the complex reasons for Seneca's failure were simplified down to the Panenka miss. There were no further questions about Cesar Fontaine, who had resigned at an emotional press conference after the match. Nothing more was said about financial misappropriation, chronic underinvestment, transfer market incompetence, or the unsustainable wage structure. The incident brought out the subtlety of the laws of cause and effect, and the backwards linearity between the two. A tragedy has no cause until it has happened. Unfairness was dispensed in gross measures, taking no account of proportionality. Panenka, guilty of one thing, had by extension become guilty of all things.

Panenka had been advised to make a statement in order to apologise or explain or otherwise have his voice included in his own story, but it was too late. He had already slipped into a deep depression and developed a dangerous indifference to himself. To describe it as sadness would be to ascribe a degree of feeling that was lacking in him during that period which lasted for – who knows? – perhaps weeks, months, or maybe almost twenty-five years.

The club had first offered Panenka a domestic loan move, before he accepted a transfer to a sister club overseas. Lauren had a million questions about it which he couldn't answer, but when the time came, the flight left without him. When his new club called him from the airport he was at home on the couch in his pyjamas watching cartoons with his daughter, and told them so. The story was reported word-for-word and served to widen his notoriety and deepen the contempt in which he was held. The day before the new season started, Panenka announced his retirement from football, aged twenty-five.

Later that year, Cesar Fontaine died from undiagnosed gallbladder cancer and was mourned with great love by the Seneca fans. He had let them down in the way that only those we love are capable of. If there was any comfort to Panenka in his disastrous penalty miss it was that it had spared Cesar's legacy. The blame for the relegation and subsequent demise of the club was forever laid at Panenka's feet, with Cesar remembered for the years he had brought inspiration and excitement to the fans and the players he had worked with. Panenka had been advised by the club, though he didn't need it explained to him, that it would be better to stay away from the funeral, a great footballing occasion that deserved better than to become a controversy. Instead, Panenka wept at home alone at the loss of his dear friend.

There is little to be said about the years that followed, during which Panenka lived like a fugitive, and in that way added to the mythology that had already started to grow up around him. He was offered coaching roles by past players of Cesar's, but declined them, and instead found work, hard work, the harder the better, wherever he could, usually with the help of his few remaining friends. But he remained disconnected, withdrawn, furtive, and committed to a slow self-destruction disguised as survival.

Lauren had appealed to Panenka too many times to leave the town, so that they could get some perspective, reclaim a small space in the world for themselves and maybe start over. But Panenka had become drunk with apathy. Whereas Lauren saw the opprobrium as an alien attack to be defended against, Panenka had already internalised the profound blame being attached to him. He deserved it and the name that had already become branded on him. The criticism was justified; the punishment similarly so. They should be allowed to destroy him, and if they didn't do it, he would do it to himself.

And so it was Lauren who carried their family during that time, and who had to face the world, bearing the judgement and pity of others. It was she who built a new life from the broken pieces of their old one. Alone, she worried about her family and about money, always money, never quite sure whether she was still in a marriage or not. But it was the grief for her plans which, over time, sapped her spirit and left her longing for the unrecoverable future she had once thought possible. Lauren's story never became part of the folklore at Seneca. It was simply one of the thousand stories that go untold in the world every day.

# Chapter 15: Esther

Marie-Thérèse and Arthur teased Panenka giddily about his hair and conducted a summary investigation into what type of barber – what type of *lady* barber, as Arthur was quick to point out, incriminatingly – would let him leave the shop like that. How could he not have known how strange he looked? Panenka was short on explanations but took comfort from being the reason for his family laughing together again. Later on, at bedtime, as Arthur was being tucked in, he admitted that he sort of liked his grandfather's new hair now that he was getting used to it.

After that night's Iron Mask, Panenka lay with his forearm across his eyebrows and thought about the breakdown in the barbershop earlier that afternoon, replaying it mindlessly like an internet video. At the time, he had said nothing for fear that he would say everything, but in spite of himself, he had been given away. Something had escaped irretrievably and yet, strangely, all he could feel was relief.

First thing the next morning, he left the Crucible and made his way back to the barbershop on the cathedral side of town, his unfinished haircut under his hat. Having persuaded himself with practical arguments about getting his hair fixed, there was no need to admit to other reasons why he might be drawn there. He entered the barbershop unsure of his welcome. She was already cutting the hair of a pensioner who must have come in early to take advantage of the midweek discounts.

'I'm a good cook, you see,' the man was saying. 'Well, I've no choice.'

'How come?' she asked.

'I'm a widower. Not that my wife was ever enthusiastic about food – she didn't grow up with it. They were a big family so food was all about hunger, not taste. Whenever we went to a rest—'

'Do you want me to trim the eyebrows and ears for you?'

'Yes please. Whenever we went to a restaurant she would say: "You order for me – I don't know what I want." Then when the food came, she'd try a bit of everything. I think she had a curiosity in her but didn't have the confidence to go with it. She was like that about most things, not only food. I miss restaurants though. I don't mind being around couples, but not in a restaurant. They're not for people on their own, are they?'

'I like to think they are,' she said. 'They give me the feeling of privacy in public. I don't really have the patience for cooking – or recipes. I tend to throw in the spices. I'd be a dangerous pharmacist.'

She showed him the back of his head in a hand mirror. He had a thin comb-over that she had managed to trim without exposing it as a lost cause.

'How's that for you?' she asked.

'Perfect. I don't like taking too much off. It's hard to know which will go first: me or the hair.'

She handed him his hat – one of those old-man jobs – and an anorak with a lavender scarf tucked into the sleeve. Panenka wondered whether it had been his wife's.

'That's perfect. I look beautiful again,' he said, leaving a tip in small coins that was more generous in intent than amount. 'I'll see you the next time, please God.'

'Bye now,' she said, with a smile that seemed to transfer from her face to his.

It was only when the man had left that Panenka realised how nervous he was.

'I like your hat. Nice colours,' she said.

'They're the Seneca colours.'

'I'm guessing that's a sports team.'

He looked at her to see if she was serious.

'It's the town's football team,' he said. 'I'd say about ninety percent of your customers are Seneca fans.'

'They must be good.'

He wasn't sure if she was being logical or joking.

'Can you fix this?' he asked, removing the hat.

'Oooh. Did I do that? I see, have a seat. The left side of your head looks good, but not on its own. Let me even you up a bit.'

He sat in the chair while she sorted through her combs and selected a pair of scissors. Watching her as she organised herself, he noticed himself noticing things. Seeing her again stabilised him.

'I don't usually do haircuts in instalments,' she said.

'I'm sorry about all that.'

With a simple hand gesture, she bid him to stop.

'I'm a sensitive person myself, so I understand,' she said.

She sprayed some water on his hair and parted it with a comb, the personal giving way to the practical.

'You've taken this place over recently haven't you?' asked Panenka.

'A couple of months ago now. It's a bit slow at times, but you hope that once people find you they'll come back, and you can build up from there. Cutting hair is all about repeat business.'

'How did you get into it?'

'An old boss of mine from a million years ago – we stayed in touch over the years and became friends. I was thinking of getting out of barbering altogether, but then when he was selling up he asked me if I was interested so I said yes. I took over the lease on his flat too, though I need to find somewhere else soon. I've never run my own place before, so we'll see how it goes. My business plan is based on the principle that hair grows in good times and in bad.'

She finished up with the scissors and ran the cut-throat over the back of his neck, brushing some hairs off with her fingers. Panenka's skin was alive to her touch.

'I honestly didn't think I'd ever see you again,' she said. 'It felt strange afterwards. I spent yesterday wondering about you. You were like this injured bird that landed in my garden and then disappeared. A story with no beginning or ending. I didn't know whether you'd flown off to safety or been eaten by a tomcat.'

'I wasn't sure whether I was doing the right thing by coming back.'

'So why did you?'

'I needed my hair finished before work.'

'That it?'

Panenka felt his impulses putting him at risk.

'You said to me... You said that you knew what it was like not to be okay,' he answered. 'And that's what *I* was left thinking about afterwards. Wondering what you meant by telling me that. I mean, I'm not expecting details or—'

'It's okay, I know what you mean.' She stood behind him with her hands on his shoulders and addressed him in the mirror. 'Do you know what resonance is?'

'Resonance?'

'It's as though one person sounds a bell in their heart, and if the other person has the same bell inside them, it rings too.'

'I see,' he said to her reflection.

'So,' she continued, 'That's how you can recognise something in someone, even if you know nothing about them. Details don't matter so much.' She put her finger on her lips: 'It's old barbershop wisdom.'

'How come Donnie never told me all this?'

'Well, wisdom is not as useful as it sounds. For one thing, it's a poor timekeeper – it doesn't usually arrive until after the fact.'

'There've been times in my life when I would have settled for wisdom after the fact,' he said.

He could smell the beeswax as she ran her fingers through his hair, styling it as she pleased.

'You know, my late father used to say: "Esther – if ever you're on a TV gameshow and they offer you two boxes – one with a prize and then another one – wisdom is what's in the other box."'

Esther. Her name was Esther.

Panenka paused.

'I'm Joseph.'

She weighed up his name, like she was consenting to it.

The noise of the hairdryer closed off their conversation as she blew the loose hairs from his neck.

Panenka got ready to leave. A draught rushed in behind them and a customer came in with it – a young man who had tied his dog to the lamppost outside where they could keep an eye on one another. He seated himself in the barber's chair without asking.

'You need to get back to work,' said Panenka.

'You look better, at least.'

'I do feel better.'

'I meant your *hair* looks better, but I'm pleased if you've cheered up.'

Her expression softened, though he couldn't have said how exactly.

'Will you be all right?' she asked. 'Out in the world, I mean.'

'I'll find out, I suppose.'

'*I won't be a sec*,' she called to the customer, who had caught her attention over Panenka's shoulder.

When she turned back to face him, he noticed that a stray hair had come out from behind her ear and was caught on the side of her mouth. He considered for a moment what it would be like to be the one who could reach out and return that hair to its place.

# Chapter 16: Screw top

Later that evening, after Marie-Thérèse had given Arthur his bath and put him to bed, she sat over a glass of unchilled white wine and a bunch of backdated magazines that Carla had brought over after receiving an SOS text. Panenka had slipped out while Marie-Thérèse was upstairs. No goodbye or explanation, which was not unusual for him, but still, she thought.

'It feels different this time,' began Marie-Thérèse. 'When my mother broke up with my dad, that was the Big Deal. That was The Event. Then, when she moved north, we had this little chat where she more or less said that I was an adult now and we should have an adult relationship, which meant me being happy for her and not looking at things from the point of view of a daughter. That she would always be my mother but that there had to come a time when she was no longer my parent.'

'I love your mother. She always says cool stuff like that. Real *mature*. They're like movie lines. My mother said to me when I moved out: "You have no idea what you have between your legs." Not exactly the kind of thing you put on a silver chain around your neck.'

'But you're close, that's the main thing.'

'So are you with yours... aren't you?'

'Sort of. I mean, yes, but... we've a lot in the bank together, and I know she's always there if I need her, but I still feel I'm on my own with this. I know what her view on staying or leaving is and, if I'm honest, I still feel a little jilted from when she left, though I'd never tell her that, obviously. Anyway, I'm not even sure if it's advice I need or maybe someone to time-travel into the future on my behalf and tell me that it all worked out fine.'

Carla topped up their wine and went over to the fridge. 'Who likes all these yoghurts and strawberry milk and all this dairy stuff?' she asked.

'Oh, Arthur eats them – my dad too. I put them in their lunchboxes.'

Carla came back to the table peeling the lid from one of Arthur's snacks: a pot of runny cheese with a compartment of salted breadsticks for dipping.

'You can't blame your mother for moving away that time, because you're your mother's daughter,' said Carla.

'What's that supposed to mean?'

'You're going to leave *me*! You're going to live up there in one of those nice modern houses, probably with real wood floors and low Japanese furniture. You'll have a little garden with all that bamboo stuff. And I bet once you get there, you'll be complaining that nothing's like it used to be and how everything changes and all that, like a big bullshitting bullshitter.'

'I'm not leaving *you*, Carla. I'd be lost without you.'

'If we were a couple, we'd be breaking up. You can't have a friendship with someone in a different town. The important rules of relationships are the same for friends as they are for boyfriends. One: stay close. Two: don't do bad shit. Three: cheering each other the fuck up. That's the basic formula. You haven't even considered our friendship.'

'Of course I have. But don't you want what's best for me? And for Arthur. I can't keep living with my dad. How would I ever move on?'

'Listen to me. Your dad is the best. I wish my dad was as nice as yours.'

'What's wrong with your dad? I think he's nice.'

'Ah, I love him and everything, but he's a smart aleck. Always has to have the last word. Always an *angle* on whatever I'm doing. Sits there in the corner, commenting on everything like one of the old geezers from the Muppets. Your dad is gentle, at least. He's got manners about him. "Hello Carla. How are you getting on with your work, Carla?" Always, always says my name. A gentleman. And another thing. He's hot. He's a good looking man, your dad is. There, I said it and I'm not ashamed. You're leaving me anyway.'

'You've been saying he's hot for years Carla. That's not new. You have this sick sort of daddy complex. Remember that weirdo, what was his name, Sam, and you used to call him "Daddy" remember? So embarrassing. You wore his shirts and everything.'

'That was a joke. He was about a year older than me, so that was our little couple gag. It wasn't even that funny.'

'Back to the important thing. I am not leaving you, Carla. There isn't another Carla in my life. I am entirely monogamous as far as Carlas go.'

'You know what I think it is. I think that you like to change things up because it's a control thing. It's a power thing.'

'You've lost me.'

'I think that you're so sick of being messed around by the important people in your life that you change things before they do. And you were only upset about your mother moving up there because she beat you to it.'

'Thank you Doctor Carla for your analysis. That brings our symposium to a close. The slides will be circulated to all participants.'

'I'm right though. As soon as things got serious with Vincent, you left home and moved in with him. Delighted about the storm it kicked up and that you had blind-sided your folks. When your mother started getting her shit together, what did you do? You resurrected your dad to show your mother that you had other options. When things started to look like they were plateauing with Vincent, like there was a pause in your life's drama for a bit – an ad break – what did you do? You split up with him for some philosophical reason that I never understood. And now you're at it again. Always shaking the snow globe. Giving yourself the *delusion* that you're in control, and letting everyone else know who's boss. Am I right?'

Marie-Thérèse sat back in her chair defensively and sloshed wine from cheek to cheek. 'Are you finished? This is starting to sound like a break-up fight.'

'Maybe it is,' said Carla. 'When you move up there, I don't want a pen pal. I'm not into virtual friendship or catch-up calls or any of that. I'm serious. I'm not mad, but we've known each other a long time, and you can't expect me to flop into your lap like a doll and say "Oh, I'm super happy for you. Live your dream, princess. Fly away little bird. Go on – off to somewhere over the rainbow." It's like I'm a small line of incidental damage on your insurance claim.'

'Are you finished?'

'I don't know. It depends if you fight back.'

'Carla, look. You're right. Not necessarily with all the psycho-analysis bit, but you're right, I haven't properly factored you into the decision. But be reasonable. How much balance can one woman sustain in the universe? I have to think of Arthur, his school and his friends; then there's Vincent; what to do with the apartment; I have work stuff going on; there's my dad, who has this weird headache thing that he won't talk about. Oh, and by the way, I am unbelievably sick of weighing up the feelings of the men in my life. I have too many umbilical cords sticking out of me. But you're right: you deserve to be treated better. Though please bear in mind that my head is already fit to explode. I need you to be a little bit of a support. I promise that before I make any decision I'll designate a whole day as "Think About Carla Day" and I'll write up on a white board all the implications for our friendship and do everything I can to make sure you and I stay like *that*,' she said, showing her first two fingers intertwined.

Carla was fishing around with the breadstick. 'Why is there never enough cheese for the breadsticks in these things?' She fixed Marie-Thérèse with something like a mafia stare. 'I would *hate* to have a boyfriend like you. You're too good at arguing. It's like you're giving in but you're actually winning. I'd love to know how to do that myself, but I don't like being on the receiving end of it.'

'If I told you I had another bottle of wine would that seal the armistice?' said Marie-Thérèse. 'It's red, though.'

'Okay. But you had to go and say "armistice," knowing that I probably wouldn't be sure what that meant. That's the kind of thing I'm talking about.'

'You're irreplaceable, Carla.'

She brought over the wine.

'What vintage is it?' asked Carla.

'Screw top.'

'My favourite.'

Marie-Thérèse poured two generous glasses, emptying half the bottle. She stood in front of the mirror and lifted up the hair behind her ear.

'Carla?'

'Yes, my disloyal friend?'

'Could you do me a quick favour...?'

# Chapter 17: Bingo's

Bingo's was what they would call in America a 'sports bar'. It had large screens on the walls like fake windows and was lit by garish blue strip lights that made the place feel like an aquarium. For all their luminescence, the lights only seemed to illuminate themselves, meaning that anyone sitting at the bar trying to read had to concentrate right at the edge of their headache threshold. Ostensibly, it was a place for watching sports but the reality was that the sports were purely there to create an atmosphere and to provide a theme for the place, along with the crucified registration plates on the walls and glass cases of what might be called memorabilia, though they belonged to nobody's memories in particular. Seneca fans never went there. It was an after-work drinking hole for unfussy water buffaloes with loosened ties; a place where loud people could hang out together like they were normal; a place where white clothes glowed and where detergent showed up on dark clothes; and a place where a middle-aged man who considered himself urbane and open minded, yet who was often disappointed by his fellow man, could read the same translation of Montaigne that he had been reading for many months, through his spare glasses with his old prescription.

It was not hard for Panenka to find BABA, who stood out at the bar like a lone burnt-out bulb.

'It's great to see Montaigne's work being read as intended: in a room full of horny thugs, under hooker lights,' said Panenka, inviting himself onto the neighbouring stool.

'Judgement of others is the hallmark of the ego,' responded BABA.

'You left your glasses behind in, shall I say, *the other place*, or is it acceptable for me to say Vincent's? I don't want to interrupt your sulk after all.'

'Thank you. I have a spare pair, but it's thoughtful of you to bring them by.'

'Where's your crème de menthe? Or don't they do it in pitchers.'

'I asked but they don't stock it here.'

'They might order it in if you're a regular. Maybe ask him,' suggested Panenka, pointing to a beefy barman who looked like he had recently finished military service.

'The staff here are taciturn. Probably because it's so loud, which makes it harder for them to engage in conversation with their customers.'

'Yeah, it is noisy. Doesn't that bother you? How can you concentrate?'

'I did ask about turning it down, but they said they're not allowed to touch the settings.'

'Couldn't you have picked somewhere else to stage your exile – what about The Crooked Clock or Abdul's?'

'Everywhere is taken.'

'How do you mean?'

'The more *conversational* hostelries are like Vincent's and have their regulars – their *lifers* – so you can't simply arrive in and declare yourself part of their conversations. It isn't how it's done.'

'You don't have to do that, but you could read at the bar like you always do and then gradually nature would take its course. It's not like you ever fully joined the conversation at Vincent's while you were there.'

'It's unnerving to have a man sitting by himself near a conversation. Naturally he will eavesdrop or at least become suspected of it. It wouldn't end well.'

Panenka ordered himself a beer and offered to buy one for BABA.

'Thank you but I'd better not. I'm not that used to beer and it makes me drunk quickly, and even a little emotional. I can handle alcohol in strength but not in volume. I usually have a light supper before going out, but it's not enough to maintain my sobriety with lager. To think of the care taken by Montaigne in his writings, but here I am with my brain having forgotten the start of a sentence by the time I reach the full stop. It's truly hopeless.'

'Why not come back to Vincent's?'

'That, I'm afraid, is equally hopeless.'

'Stop being a baby. You could go back with me this evening and sit in your usual spot and we'd all be glad to see you – even Anthony. He wouldn't admit it, but everyone knows he misses you. You're the Anti-Anthony. Without you he has nothing to stand against.'

'Anthony is miserable and consequently sees misery everywhere he looks. He is like a man who salts his food before he tastes it and then complains that everything tastes the same.'

'I can't disagree, but you have to look past all that. His marriage is unhappy and he's a bit worn out by everything. We need to accept him as he is.'

'Panenka, I respect you. You have – I hope you don't mind me saying – you have been through *a lot*. I've no difficulty with you, as I hope you know. But I can guarantee you that I have absolutely accepted Anthony as he is. If I thought I could change him I would never have left Vincent's. But things being as they are, he will remain his self-pitying old self, and he will not be happy until everyone around him is as miserable as he is. But even that will not make him satisfied.'

'I think that's harsh. It's not simply his outlook, which I agree is a bit on the bleak side, but he is dealing with personal difficulties that would puncture anyone's hope.'

'Latterly, that is the case, but he has been that way since always. I know the type of person he is. He is opinionated in the worst possible way. He carries within him – in his mind – a world view that is as carefully constructed and beloved as a model railway set. Everywhere he goes he will orientate the conversation to create an opening for people to admire the model railway set in his head. He seeks out validation for his railway and panics whenever a heavy boot of reality comes stomping near it. There is no exchange of ideas with that man. For all his jousting and mental foreplay, he is incapable of change. His worldview might depress him but at least it's familiar, and for a man in crisis, that's often enough.'

Panenka recognised something in what he heard.

'What do you have in your head then? Are you telling me that all the blame lies with old Eeyore Anthony?'

'I consider myself a student and have the humility that goes with that. At least I'm curious about new ideas. I have an open mind, but not an empty mind. Of course, I have my flaws, chief among which is my sensitivity. Perhaps if I were more resilient I would not be here in this awful place.'

'I'm relieved to hear you say it's awful.'

They left Bingo's several hours later, though it was hard to judge time in a blue-lit world with no circadian prompts. BABA, it was clear, could not hold his drink, or at least could not hold beer. They had ended up sharing a pitcher, but once BABA started lecturing about Montaigne in a slurred, roundabout way, Panenka made sure not to top him up any further.

On the way home, Panenka kept watch as BABA urinated behind a skip in a side lane. 'Cold tonight, isn't it?' said BABA as he was doing it, speaking for both himself and his exposed organ.

'I'd better take you back to your place,' said Panenka. 'It wouldn't do for you to walk home alone on our first date. What would your father say?'

'My father was a kind man. There are many men who get to my age and who carry their fathers around in their heads – trying to be as like them, or unlike them, as possible. But me, I had a decent father. Dead now of course, but he did his best.'

They reached BABA's apartment building, which looked like a form of social housing or old folks' complex. The bricks were the colour of dog food and the windows had flaky wooden semi-circles under the ledges, like bags under their eyes. The building was a squat three storeys and had no lift. 'No fire escape either,' said BABA. 'Need to be a light sleeper and a good jumper if there's an emergency.'

BABA struggled with the key, which was on a keyring attached to the loop on his trousers – he was trying to open the door by standing on his tippy toes, pushing his pelvis near the handle.

'Here, let me,' said Panenka. 'My God, how many keys have you got? Are you a jailer in a fairy castle or something?'

'It's the one with the blue ... the blue *thing* on it,' said BABA.

Panenka opened the front door, which was more like an inside door, and patted around the wall for a light. He helped carry BABA in, shoulder-to-shoulder, World War I style. The main living room was a scene of disgusting chaos and domestic incompetence. Newspapers were stacked on the floor and in a bucket on an armchair. There were half-eaten apples and black bananas lying on surfaces. Clothes were scattered throughout, as though the ghosts who had been wearing them had expired when the door opened. The furniture was worn and musty, with old lamps and half-deconstructed electrical objects abandoned around the place. Beside the door was a plant pot of loose change, made up of different currencies, including a few coins that had holes in the middle of them. At first Panenka thought there was only one room, but then he noticed a balcony overhanging the wall behind him, where BABA's bed had been moved somehow up the narrow uncarpeted staircase.

'My apologies for the mess. The UN was due to send a cleaner over,' said BABA as he sat back on a pile of clothes that had an armchair underneath them.

Panenka went out through the hall to find the kitchen and fetch BABA a glass of water. He found foil take-away boxes stacked on the floor and dishes were piled at odd angles in the sink half-filled with scummy water. There was an uncut loaf of tiger cob on a bread board; it was crusty in a bad way. He opened the cupboards to find them largely empty: one or two clean plates and a couple of souvenir mugs. He filled one, letting the tap run first, and brought it back in to where BABA was dozing.

'Does anyone ever call here, BABA? Have you any family or neighbours?'

'*I am a rock, I am an iiii-yi-yi-laaand*,' sang BABA, as he collapsed back on the chair.

'Maybe you could use a bit of help. It's not easy doing everything yourself.'

Panenka sat down opposite him, the room lit by the low-watt bulb in the hall and by the streetlights that shone, unobstructed, through the uncurtained windows. BABA looked like he was starting to fall asleep but Panenka didn't want to leave him.

'Come on, I promise, it's always worth the effort of making it to bed,' he said as he pulled BABA by his sleepy arm out of the chair.

'Panenka, you never told me whether they bought that damn TV at Vincent's,' said BABA, with a melancholy smile.

'Let's not discuss politics at this late hour,' said Panenka, who had some small success in getting BABA's top half to cooperate, even if his legs dragged a little on the stairs.

He laid BABA on the bed and took off his jacket and his shoes. Then he lifted the heavy woollen blankets over him and tucked him in a bit

'We'll let you off brushing your teeth tonight,' he said. 'Special treat. Don't try going downstairs until the morning, unless you need the toilet, but be careful.'

'Thank you – you are a lady and a gentleman,' said BABA in a dreamy voice, though the humour had gone from it.

Panenka took BABA's glasses off and folded them on top of his Montaigne on the bedside table. The streetlight hardly reached the balcony, but Panenka noticed a set of matching frames hanging above the bed.

'Look at that,' he said, as BABA stared up at him sadly. 'Turns out you do have two degrees after all.'

# Chapter 18: Raining Indoors

Panenka arrived at the café a few minutes early. He and Esther had started to meet during those offcuts of time that appear, uncounted, in every day: a coffee in the morning before Panenka's shift, a walk around the block after the barbershop closed. One lunch hour, he had brought her a pastry to have with her tea, and stayed to keep her company during the early afternoon lull. In this way she had made space for him without making him ask, and they had become comfortable with each other.

The lease on the flat where Esther was staying was almost up and she needed to find somewhere soon, so she asked Panenka to meet her for a coffee to get his views on her shortlist – her main priority was to avoid a murder house or somewhere next to a prison or sewage plant. She had chosen a nice high-ceilinged café that Panenka had not been in for many years, not since his habits had settled. It had a glass atrium, with light and effervescent table talk filling the room as rain drummed on the glass above their heads. There was wood panelling on the walls and large unframed abstract paintings hung around the place, the type of art Panenka didn't understand. It wasn't much like Vincent's.

He had been seated at a small round table, the legs of which forced his knees to butterfly out uncomfortably close to the young man beside him, who was scrolling through his phone over a bowl of sweet-smelling soup. They were as tight as aeroplane seats.

Esther arrived and cast a look around before seeing Panenka's waving hand, which brushed against his neighbour's shoulder briefly, for which they both made mechanical apologies. She was wearing a burgundy leather jacket, fitted jeans and black musketeer boots up to her knees; her hair was a little wet from the rain in a way that suited her. The silver necklace she wore was shaped like a crescent on its back and flashed as the light glanced off it. Panenka was glad he had worn the dark shirt and herringbone jacket he had bought for his fiftieth, when Marie-Thérèse had booked a meal for them all at a nice steak place.

'Busy, isn't it?' she said, 'And loud! It's like a schoolyard.' She registered a look at the young man in the neighbouring seat. 'It's normally so much quieter. I come in here sometimes and sit with my book and a pot of tea to pass away an hour or two. I've never seen it like this.'

'It's because of the parade,' said their neighbour, without looking up from his phone. 'Or not parade, a demonstration. It's for extremists and people who don't like extremists I think. It's ridiculous if you ask me. No offence if you're extremists or anything, but I parked my bike against a signpost on a street that's been closed off and now I can't get it back until the whole thing is over.'

'It's fine. We're not extremists. Pity about your bike – at least you're in out of the rain,' said Esther.

'I'm trying to look on the positive and enjoy a little downtime, but to be honest it's inconvenient for me. I've an essay to finish and I'm way behind.'

Esther extricated herself and turned to Panenka.

'You look nice,' she said. 'Should we order?'

'I'll have a coffee.'

'Nothing to eat?'

'You said we were meeting for coffee so I ate before I came out. Did I misunderstand you?'

'What did you have?'

'Eggs.'

'Just eggs?'

'Yeah, scrambled eggs. Why are you looking at me like that?'

'Nothing – I admire your simple taste.' She stifled a smile.

Panenka was confused – were eggs a bad thing or not?

Their neighbour offered his own thoughts. 'I ordered the beetroot soup. I don't know why exactly, as I haven't had beetroot in years. I'm not into pickled vegetables and all that, no offence. We had them a lot growing up. But this is different – almost rich, like a dessert.' He was running bread around the side of his bowl like it was competing in a NASCAR race.

Esther ordered and their neighbour took the opportunity to settle his own bill, which he paid with coins carefully counted from a little clamshell purse.

'I don't believe in tipping,' he said in a lowered voice after the waiter had left. 'They factor it into the price anyway.' He bid them a captain's salute as he left.

'Bye,' she said in a voice that faded after him. 'That guy was strange, wasn't he? What would he have said if I had answered that we were extremists? Is that the kind of thing people own up to?'

She took out a plastic folder with some rental ads she had printed, and spread them out on the table.

'So,' she began, 'the first thing I need to know is which are the areas to avoid, then after that I can think about what other compromises I'll have to make. It's been such a long time since I've had to do this – I forgot how much I hated it.'

'I haven't been house hunting in years myself – where are you interested in?'

'Anywhere near the barbershop looks too expensive,' she said, showing him an ad for a small flat with a view of the cathedral.

'I didn't know things had become so pricey,' he said. 'I would have thought you could get a room *in* the cathedral for that rent.'

'Probably best not to live too close to the shop anyway, otherwise I'll never get to know the town. What about this?'

'That's at the Seneca end – see this on the map? That's the stadium – you might have people peeing on your front door every second Saturday. There's nothing on that side of town anyway except bars and take-aways.'

He looked across at her. She was over-concentrating, the line of her neck accentuated as she angled her head to read the ad.

'What about this one – where's that area?' she asked. 'It seems to be near the Metro at least, maybe even walkable. Cheap too.'

'I don't think so.'

'Is it rough?'

'It's... it's near where I live. It's an area called the Crucible.'

Their order arrived. His coffee was served in a cobalt blue mug the size of a bowl, with a tiny handle – he lifted it like a schoolmaster pulling a student by the ear. Her cake was a creamy conch and looked like it would be impossible to eat with dignity, though fun to watch her try.

'Are you sure you don't want to share this monster?' she offered.

'I'd better not,' he said.

'Are you afraid that if I share my cake you'll have to share your neighbourhood?'

'It's not that. You see, the Crucible is a pretty run-down part of town. I'm used to it, but you might prefer somewhere nicer. I mean, you deserve somewhere nicer.'

'Would it be safe?'

'Oh, well, yes, I think so. I've no worries about Arthur playing on the street or anything.'

Esther, who was sawing her cake with the side of her fork, paused at the unfamiliar name.

'Sorry, that's my grandson.'

'A grandson?' she asked. 'I assume you have children then – or did you go straight to having grandchildren?'

'I've one daughter – Marie-Thérèse, who's an adult now. Too much so at times – carries the whole world with her wherever she goes. She's doing very well – she's recently been promoted to manager at the supermarket. Her mother and I split up a long time ago and her son, Arthur, is my grandson. They live with me. Here, I'll show you.'

He passed her the picture of Arthur on his phone's home screen.

'That's old – one of his baby pictures,' he said.

'Ah yes, he was still landscape then,' she said. 'He's probably portrait now.'

'He's seven. He already thinks he runs the town. How about you – any children?'

She shook her head without elaboration. His instinct to open up about his family shrank back within him. It didn't feel right to outnumber her.

Their waiter excused himself and asked if he could move them for a moment. The rain had started to leak from the atrium roof and was pooling behind them. Esther apologised in that needless way people do to smooth over something awkward. They stood side by side watching the waiters mopping up and milling around. He had let her judge the distance between them, and could feel how close she was. There was a note of incense in her perfume.

'It's funny, you surprised me then,' she said in a lowered voice. 'You're a real person aren't you? With your own other life and history and everything. You're not just a robot who goes limp when I leave the room. I suppose I overlooked that you've had a whole life that has brought you to this point. I mean, we become who we are, right?'

He gestured in a supposing way.

She continued: 'I'm not sure I put too much faith in a person's life story though – the stuff that's happened to them. If I met an old school friend and they asked me what I'd been up to for the past twenty years I could probably tell them in a few sentences. But if they asked me what had gone through my head that morning, I could keep them talking all day. Which of those is what's "happening" to a person, really – the outside stuff or the inside stuff?'

'Can you really know somebody without knowing a bit of both?' he suggested.

'Well, look at us. I could have asked for the full tour – you could have shown me around all your own facts and circumstances, given me the tourist board version of yourself. A whole story that I would later have to revise or unlearn based on who you turned out to be. But if I start with what you're actually like, pick you up where I found you, then at least I'm starting with *my* information. I can sketch you my own way, and then colour you in over time. And you could do the same with me.'

The phrase 'over time' caught his ear.

'I'll be honest,' he said. 'These days, I don't find myself getting to know too many new people. Most of my friends are old friends. I'm out of practice with all those strategies you're talking about. I'm happy to let time do the work. And time with you feels different to any other type of time.'

Panenka looked across at her, standing there in a room full of words. He could feel the difference between who he was alone and who he was when he was with her. The rain, outside and inside, was complicit in their intimacy.

The waiter broke in with more apologies and re-seated them, changing the chemistry of the moment. The room sounded loud again and their conversation returned to the practicalities of real estate and all the other things two people can find to talk about.

# Chapter 19: Homework

'Okay Arthur, you can have a few minutes of TV and then we'll get stuck into the homework,' said Vincent.

'Let's get it out of the way,' said Arthur, dropping his bag onto the kitchen table like the burden it was.

'What do you have in this bag that it's so heavy?'

'Ah, the usual. Books and stuff.'

'A full dictionary, two hardback encyclopaedias, a maths workbook,' itemised Vincent, looking into the bag, which belched a nauseating smell of crayons. 'That's too much for a boy your age to carry. Do you want me to write a note asking if you can leave them in school? And look, you never ate your fruit or your other bread roll – did you not get a second break today?'

'I did. They don't give us enough time. They always rush us.'

'Do you want me to talk to your teacher?'

'It's okay. Do you know what my teacher says about you?'

'Eh... what?'

'She says you're her neighbour.'

'Oh, okay,' said Vincent, relieved. 'Yeah, she must live on this block somewhere.'

They were at Vincent's apartment, which had also been Arthur's apartment until he had moved out with his mother the year before. Vincent had been hoping that this was a temporary arrangement and so had kept everything unchanged, including Arthur's room, which was decorated in baby blue or, as Arthur called it disparagingly, 'Babygro blue.' A few of his clothes and toys were kept there, though a year is another lifetime for a seven-year-old, and he had already outgrown anything that had been left behind.

Vincent was always careful not to allow an accretion of bachelorhood into the place: beer bottles were recycled as they were used, and there were no lapses into movie posters or cheap bedspreads. Whenever Marie-Thérèse called over to collect Arthur, she would stay at the front door instead of coming in, though Vincent chose not to read whatever message that was meant to convey.

'Right, let's see what we have in your journal today. "Read two pages from *History in Our Time*" – that's easy enough. "Then take five words and put them into sentences" – it doesn't say which five words.'

'They're on the next page – here, I'll show you.'

'Let's see: *flower, grower, shower, pow–*'

'Let me do it! You check it at the end. I'll write out all the sentences first.'

'Fine. Can you think of a sentence with flower in it?'

'I can't think of anything.'

'You didn't give yourself a chance. What do you know about flowers?'

'Flowers are nice?'

'Come on, you can do better than that. Think of something that happened to you to do with flowers. Does Mama have flowers at home?'

*'Mama has flowers at home.'*

'Does she? Did she buy them herself, or do you know if someone else bought them for her?'

'She doesn't have flowers. I was lying for my homework.'

'Got it, right. Go with that sentence. Write *Mama has flowers at home that Daddy bought her.*'

'I'm not writing that.'

'Fine then. Write *Mama has flowers at home.*'

Arthur got down to it, his tongue sticking out as he concentrated.

'Remember to use a finger space between the words—'

'We don't do that any more.'

'—and *Mama* has a capital 'M' doesn't it, because she's important to us all, isn't she?'

'It's not her real name, though.'

'Yeah, I know. But it's like a name, which means it gets a capital letter. Next up is *grower*. Can you think of anything for that? Think of what grows.'

'Children grow.'

'They do indeed. You're always growing aren't you? You're going to be taller than me, I bet. Any ideas for a sentence?'

'*I will be the biggest grower in my family*.'

'I see what you mean, but that's not how that word works.'

'I do grow myself. In my sleep.'

'That's true.'

'Nobody else is growing me. I grow myself.'

'Again, you're not wrong.'

'*I am the grower of myself*. Done.'

They carried on through the rest of the homework, bargaining and compromising. Vincent didn't mind these little skirmishes: they gave him a chance to spar with Arthur and kept him in touch with what was happening in his world.

'Who did you play with in school today?' he asked.

'I don't remember.'

'Was it Daniel, Charlie, Jake, the other boy with red hair, Matthew is it?'

'Matteo. He's sick this week. He has jungle fever.'

'Are you sure that's what he has?'

'Yes!'

'It sounds made up.'

'That's what he has. His brother has an iguana. And he smokes.'

'The iguana or the brother?'

'The brother. Iguanas don't smoke.'

Between homework and parent-teacher meetings he was confident that he could piece together a picture of Arthur as a bright, if slightly over-relaxed student; maybe even the good type of lazy, like the super smart children who stop trying because of boredom and then go on to become teenage millionaires. The schoolyard, though, was where Arthur's social future would be foreshadowed. Children tended not to care about each other's parents, whether they were married, separated, divorced or even dead. But Vincent wondered about other parents. He and Marie-Thérèse had stayed outside the network of arrangements that were transacted at the school gates – play dates, sleepovers and the like. They were an insular family, which was fine so long as they were happy, but now they were living apart Vincent started to wonder why Arthur seemed to go to fewer birthday parties these days. Were the kids starting to grow out of all that or were separated parents too political a prospect for inclusion – which parent to ask, who is Arthur even living with? All that stuff.

'Arthur?'

'Yup?'

'Is anyone bullying you?'

'Nope.'

'Are you sure? You can always tell me. Daddies have big ears for listening.'

'I said nope,' whispered Arthur.

'Sure?' Vincent whispered back.

'Yes!' Arthur shouted, smiling. 'Why are people always asking me about bullies? Adults are obsessed with bullies. Teachers keep talking about them, Mama keeps talking about them. Why are you so terrified of bullies? They're just kids.'

Having finished his homework, more or less, Arthur went over to the cupboard and took out a yoghurt-coated rice cake and leapt onto the couch, landing bum first in a seated position. They sat together watching the afternoon's TV, Arthur manoeuvring across the arm of Vincent's chair and into his lap, where he half sat/half lay in front of the screen, sucking on the aglet from the cord on his tracksuit bottoms. Vincent played with Arthur's hair, idly spiking it into a Mohawk and then flattening it down again.

'We need to get you a haircut, my friend,' said Vincent.

Arthur moved Vincent's hand away and flattened his hair back to the way he liked it.

The cartoons were American: fast, flashy scenes, with humour full of pop culture references – made for children but with the idea of impressing adults. Arthur watched them impassively, saying out loud from time to time that something was funny without actually laughing at it.

'Listen, can I ask you something?' said Vincent.

'Let me think about it.'

'Do you ever want to talk to me about Mama and Daddy?'

'No thanks.'

'I'm always here.'

'Can we get a bearded dragon?'

'Not that sort of question.'

'They're not dragons. They're lizards.'

'I understand, but can we talk about that another time?'

'Well then, you're not helping. I'm probably going to be bullied for not having one.'

Arthur increased the volume on the TV as Vincent went to the kitchen and checked the fridge, knowing that the evening's menu would be reported back to Marie-Thérèse. She would want to know whether he was playing the popularity game by filling Arthur with junk and leaving her to handle the five-a-day. It was a test of how responsible he was towards Arthur and how fair he was being towards her. He understood all that just like the way he understood that the separation was an opportunity to bring perspective to a relationship that had buckled under the exhaustion and demands of parenthood. The basic equation of life involved variables like money, rest, spare time – time of any sort – enthusiasm, curiosity, and above all, energy. Once the equilibrium in a relationship was lost, there was no self-correcting mechanism, except to turn the whole thing off for a while in the hope that it would restore itself on reactivation. Vincent had no choice but to accept the separation without any promises about where things would go next, if anywhere. The split had been definite without being definitive. It was clear that Marie-Thérèse wanted time apart, but she showed no signs of moving on and he had not yet been able to decode her frosty reactions. Sometimes it seemed like a declaration of hurt, other times a need for space. Vincent had been patient, and had decided that he would stay that way until things were less opaque, even though there was part of him that worried he was confusing doubt with hope. After all, a few crumbs of love could be made to last a long time if they are all you have.

In the bleakest terms, he now stood to lose everything. If Marie-Thérèse moved north with Arthur, it would be for a new beginning without him. He wasn't yet sure whether she had fully decided to go, or whether this was a warning shot to provoke him into saving their relationship. Certainly, the separation had not produced the settling down he had hoped for; it had simply made their love rusty, and perhaps rusty beyond repair. But it was hard to fix a relationship he had been happy with. There was no source of dissatisfaction on his part to trigger his creativity and problem-solving. All he had was a general impressionistic sense that Marie-Thérèse was unhappy and his part in that. In his most doubtful moments he had wondered whether, if he loved her truly, he should accept her decision if the alternative was to stand in the way of her peace. And then there was Arthur.

Vincent had always been close to Arthur. He was quietly relieved when they finally decided to bottle feed after he was born. Those first few days had been exhausting for Marie-Thérèse and when Arthur wouldn't latch on, the feeds became interminable for her. The bottle had allowed Vincent to become close to his new son and their relationship had been forged during those night time feeds; a bond based on body heat, smell and satisfying Arthur's primal needs while his exhausted mother recovered her strength. In those early years Vincent had worked a variety of manual jobs: a bakery, outdoor painting, maintenance gardener, and spells in factories doing shift work, sometimes at night. He had always found shift work hard, but the pattern of working three or four days on then three days off meant that he could often spend time at home with his young child. When Marie-Thérèse first went back to work after her maternity leave, he remembered the serious sound of the door as it closed, leaving him home with this tiny, busy bundle for the day. The minutes and hours stretched and he struggled at first to persevere through the psychological tiredness that sapped the joy that was theoretically central to parenthood. It was routine that saved him. The day became divided up into hour-long or fifteen-minute segments: feeds and changes, walks and then more walks, or calling in on Panenka, whose own shifts often left him free during the day.

When Vincent had first started seeing Marie-Thérèse, there was no mention of Panenka, whom Vincent had known about separately through the folklore of Seneca FC, the team he had followed since he was a boy. At that stage Marie-Thérèse was living at home with her mother and, while she was open with him, all she had said was that her father was away a lot when she was young and that he and her mother were no longer together. There was something practised in the way she summarised her father's part in her life. Vincent had inadvertently found out that she was Panenka's daughter when he met an old friend at a bar one night after a Seneca game, and they got talking about their lives. The friend had been in the same school as Marie-Thérèse and explained how she was known to everyone as her father's daughter, which had brought with it a perverse mix of infamy and awe. It was always the first thing thrown back at her by anyone she didn't get along with.

Vincent hadn't told Marie-Thérèse that he knew who her father was, and when she eventually opened up about it, providing an abridged personal history, it was as though she were both confessing a secret and defending him. She explained that after Panenka left Seneca in such difficult circumstances as a young man, Lauren had always told her that he needed to travel to earn money and assured her that he rang every night after Marie-Thérèse was asleep to say how much he missed them. Panenka would leave the house periodically, but would often disappear without saying goodbye, sometimes for weeks at a time, before returning without explanation. Marie-Thérèse recalled one time, when she was about eleven, and had been told, fancifully, that Panenka was away working on an oil rig in the middle of a stormy sea. She had been cycling home from a friend's house and had stopped at a shop to buy a carton of milk for her mother. At the door of the shop she froze on seeing Panenka in the queue in front of her. If she had truly believed her mother's stories wouldn't she have run up to him, delighted by the surprise? But some other truth had already made a nest in her heart, and seeing that alternative become a reality was too much for her. She ran back to her bike and raced home, where she went straight to her room, leaving the milk money in the hall and her mother calling after her. Having told Vincent this while perched on the edge of the bus stop bench, Marie-Thérèse turned and looked at him directly and warned him not to draw conclusions. He had pulled her close and said nothing. It was one of only a handful of vulnerable moments she had allowed herself in all the time they had been together.

Years later, when Marie-Thérèse was pregnant with Arthur, she had invited Panenka to meet for a coffee alone. Vincent had never been told what they discussed, whether it was a comprehensive reckoning, or a storing away of accumulated grievances. With a graciousness that proved, if proof were needed, the invulnerability of Marie-Thérèse's goodness, she admitted Panenka back into her life, and that of her new family. On those exhausted mornings when Vincent arrived at Panenka's house with Arthur teething and biting on a teaspoon to cool his gums, Panenka had been happy to take his grandson onto his chest and walk him up and down the stairs singing Old Man River or any other baritone song, so that the vibrations would comfort or distract a baby who had no idea that teething pain would pass. Vincent would sit a moment and, as he would admit freely, indulge in a survival nap, hardly believing that the man so central to a notorious piece of Seneca folklore was able to perform such magic to relieve his child.

As Vincent fussed around the house, cooking dinner for Arthur and waiting for Marie-Thérèse to pick him up, he was shadowed by the thought of losing all this. Losing the people in his life and the history he had with them. It was surely too impossible to even allow the thought into his home. While he stirred pasta in his distracted state, across the room on the countertop where his phone was charging, a message came in for him:

> Sorry – had to work late – can you hang on for another hour? MT

Vincent tried to remember when it was that Marie-Thérèse had stopped signing messages with kisses.

# Chapter 20: Walking the Crucible

Panenka took the barbershop route after work to pick up Esther for the walk around the Crucible he had promised.

'I'll just be a minute finishing up here. Have you ever used one of these before?' she asked, handing him a sweeping brush.

Though not formally trained, he cleared up a small pile of donkey-coloured hair while she bagged the takings and sterilised her scissors and combs in a container of murderous-sounding blue liquid called Barbicide.

'What do you do with all the hair?' he asked.

'What do you mean?'

'Does it go in the bin or what?'

'What else did you think we did with it?'

'I don't know. I thought you might recycle it or something.'

Esther paused to picture this, but couldn't.

'How was business today?' he asked

'I'm struggling to find my rhythm. If you're working for somebody else you don't mind a few quiet periods, but with your own place you fret when it's empty and then again when there are queues. And there's less of this than I thought there'd be,' she said, pointing to the money in the till. 'I hope I don't end up working for debt. Here – use this,' she said, handing him a dustpan.

He hadn't considered what it was like for her, being the person who had to think of everything.

'Sorry,' she said, 'I'm riding my energy these days. When it's low, I'm low. I'll be fine once we're out.'

She locked up and they cut across town rather than taking the Metro, Esther linking his arm. Panenka was used to walking alone with all the intent of a man trying to outpace his own thoughts, but being with Esther forced him to walk the way she walked: with her head up and pivoting towards the stimuli. She was an ostentatious watcher, staring with impunity the way a child does. He realised she must see a very different town to the one he knew.

'How do you get away with staring like that?' he asked.

'I need it. I like absorbing the noise and the light and the faces. I photosynthesise it all. It restores my energy after the day. Don't you like to connect with people?'

'I prefer to be a stranger among strangers. It gives me the superpower of invisibility.'

'I get that. Eye contact is a big commitment for some people; but I like to know I'm surrounded by life. I don't like the thought of being a lit room in a dark house.'

To Panenka that was exactly how she seemed.

He took her off into the Crucible. The flats in the area were small, which tended to flush life out onto the street and into the community, externalising domestic situations. People were used to seeing family arguments, friends falling out and couples breaking up, all in a form of unscripted street theatre. In a strange way it made gossip pointless when there was no secret about what people were really like.

They passed some men leaning elbows on their taxi roofs, disputing something and numbering their points on their fingers. Two men stood nearby outside a fish shop, hosing blue plastic crates with a power washer, discussing women. A mother was either reprimanding or pleading with her teenage daughter from a first floor apartment window, though the girl on the street below hardly looked up from her phone. A young boy, wearing a yellow t-shirt in the evening humidity, was absent-mindedly kicking a ball against a shop gable, chatting to a girl who was sitting on a wheelie bin and watching him. At a bus stop they passed a young woman crying on her phone and listening miserably to whatever she was being told. Around a corner they swerved around an elderly woman who stood and steadied herself against a post box while her husband tied her shoelace for her. A dinnertime smell hung in the air. It came from nowhere in particular but seemed to be everywhere, a mix of oil and spices and something else – onions maybe, but not just onions. Esther took it all in.

He had not been joking about the Crucible's limited appeal. It really was an agglomeration of grim flats and rentals, with all the random commerce that goes with personal transience. And yet he wanted to show it to her, and she wanted to see it. Before the Iron Mask, Panenka had for years navigated through these streets by himself, looping around and cutting through other parts of town whenever that seemed like the thing to do. The walks were his way of burning off the emotional calories built up from over-processing his own obsessions. He preferred the area late at night, after the cafés and bars had closed, when the chairs had been stacked and taken in from the pavements and the bottles had been filed into crates, ready to be collected the next morning. The only people around would be late night workers heading home for a bad night's sleep, or street people with their own crazy business to mind. Back then, his habits had worried Lauren, but he had always felt safer going out at those obscure times. It was what he did instead of sleep.

Alongside Esther now, as the day ripened into evening, it felt like he was walking through a different place. The usual atmospheric pressure dissolved in her presence as the baked brown light bounced off the jaded sandstone buildings. He hadn't planned a tour for her. It was an undesigned part of town, built one era at a time, a creature of incremental compromises, and it was best to explore it in that same undeliberate spirit. There was no natural centre, there were no blocks or grids, and there was no obvious circuit that would bring a walker back to their starting point. It wasn't difficult to get lost in it, or to lose others. By simply following the rhythm of alternating right and left feet, it was possible to walk turn by turn, crossing by crossing, without any real appreciation of distance or time.

'This is proving surprisingly refreshing,' she said. 'I haven't mapped the town out in my head yet – I keep using the same few routes for everything. I'm like that train at the zoo that's happy to ride the same track all day.'

'How come you chose to come here?' he asked. 'This is a town that people leave and leave behind, unless you've nowhere else to go. But you're not like that. You've got a handle on things – you could do better.'

'It wasn't a force of attraction necessarily. I thought that this is a place where nobody knows me and where it would be okay for me to fail. There was safety in that. I could make mistakes here and there would be no witnesses. And I needed that until I regained my faith in myself.'

She checked herself as a couple walked between them in silence.

'Sorry, I don't mean to get heavy,' she said when they had passed.

But the way she talked didn't feel heavy at all. She was open in ways that he was not, but cryptic in ways that he recognised.

'What's your reason for staying?' she asked. 'How come you still live here? It can't be all that much of a dump.'

'I wish I had a good answer for that,' he said. 'At times this place has been like quicksand. At other times like the centre of the world. I'm not even sure how much of this town is still in me, and what would be left of me if I were ever to move away. Is there even a safe way to find that out?'

'You're not unhappy here though, are you?'

'I never thought I was happy here,' he said, eventually. 'But I suppose I must have been. Why else did I stay?'

It amazed him that she could make him find new questions to ask about the place.

'You must have a lot of love for it though. I mean, you've been monogamous with the town for half a century.'

'That's a complicated question for me. After all, a town is just a town. But I'll admit I wanted you to like it. I was curious about how you two would get along.'

'You say it like you're introducing me to your family.'

Just as he was about to answer about his family, he changed his mind. He liked to think of Esther as a separate solar system where there were no linkages, no past, no context, no accumulation, no connections, no disconnections. It was jarring to think about introducing her to the other side of his life.

'You don't mention your family much,' she said.

They stopped to let two men in front of them lift a torn, moss green couch from the kerbside into a van. It almost looked like they were stealing it.

'What does it say about us that we're so slow to talk about the people in our lives?' she asked, having had a minute to think about it.

A quiet grew between them as they resumed walking. They turned through a side street onto the town's main artery, and climbed the metal steps of the pedestrian overpass. Their feet made a hammering sound on the way up, and the bridge wobbled a little above the traffic that gushed underfoot. The sides of the bridge were not solid but caged in an arrangement of bars and mesh they could see through. It curved over their heads to form a functional tunnel, presumably as a safety precaution, though the noise and wind around them created a feeling of vulnerability on all sides. Esther stopped and leaned on her forearms against the bars, looking at the retreating car lights, which changed from white to red once they passed under the bridge. A low, porridgey moon was staring at them over silhouetted hills.

'You asked me why I had moved here,' she said. 'I came here to start again, Joseph.'

Panenka leaned on the bar beside her.

'For twelve years I lived with my boyfriend. The man who was supposed to be the rest of my life. His name is Eugene. In its fullest form, it's a long story, but the essence of it takes only a few words: he cheated on me. I remember him using the word "unfaithful" as though it were something quaint and dignified. Throughout those twelve years he'd had other relationships, some of them possibly close and serious. I didn't discover this by myself: he had to tell me. Like most people my greatest strength is my greatest weakness, which in my case means I have faith in people. I trust instinctively, like a child, instead of figuring out the risks. He said he wanted to clear the weeds in his past to make a path for our future, and I'm sure someday I'll find the bad poem he stole those words from. When I think back, I really hated the way he used language. Always choosing big concepts to convey small, selfish little ideas.'

Panenka passed her his hat to dry her eyes on.

'We nearly broke up a few years ago. By then, my friends, or at least the friends who were in relationships, had started their families. I told him that I could wait for almost anything but that I was ready to have children. It wasn't like any other want I've ever had. It wasn't an ambition or about *having* something I didn't already have. It was like there was a part of me unexpressed. But Eugene simply said no. He said that he had come to understand what he wanted from the relationship and that it didn't include any more children. He hardly saw the two he already had with his ex. It didn't matter what we had discussed before, he came to this realisation himself, and *by* himself. He said he was asking me to come on what he kept calling a "life journey" together. What could I do? I loved him so I decided to let that ambition go, not that you ever truly give it up. You simply disguise it as an imitation of satisfaction.

'So I stayed.

'I stayed and grieved inside that relationship. Telling myself that I had made the type of compromise that adults make. And now it's over and my chance to ever experience that is gone. It's like there's a space inside me where a tooth has been pulled and the gum is soft and sore around it. I could say so much about how unfair it all is, and how I wasted myself on the wrong person, but there's nowhere to bring that pain. And anyway, you still need to put your life somewhere. You still need to put yourself somewhere.'

Panenka reached over and stroked her fingers. 'You didn't deserve to be treated like that, Esther,' he said.

'And then, months after we broke up, he emailed me with this rambling, selfish essay, practically forgiving me for leaving, if you can believe that, but hoping that I would find happiness, as if I were waiting for his blessing. Then he casually drops in that he and his new partner were expecting a baby; as though it were an incidental fact that I might be curious about.

'I still feel wounded. It's like he fired an arrow through the one little loophole of unexplored vulnerability I had left. I don't know whether I was angry at him, or frustrated that he could still reach me from a distance. But I came to a decision. I refuse to live as an incomplete person. I *will* get over this. I am determined to. I plan to live to be a hundred and those twelve years will seem like nothing.'

Esther's voice broke as she dabbed her eyes with Panenka's hat. She turned around and leaned her back on the bars to look at him. The breeze blew her hair around her face. She let it flicker about her.

'That's how it is. You go from investing your plans in someone to being nobody at all. A woman of no status. So, after a while I left and came here and started this business because I didn't know what else to do with myself.'

Panenka took her into his arms and let her sorrow sink into him. He kissed the top of her head and then rested his chin there.

'Sometimes, as I get older,' she said, 'I wonder whether all that's left are the unfixable things.'

# Chapter 21: Bedtime

'Knock!' shouted Arthur.

'I wanted to check in case you needed anything,' said Marie-Thérèse through the bathroom door.

'Knock, I said!'

'Is the water too hot?'

'I'm already finished.'

'Then how come the shower is still running?'

'I couldn't reach the thing – can you do it?'

'Sure, but can I come in?'

'Wait – I have to tie the towel around my tummy... Right, come on in.'

Marie-Thérèse had been trying to get Arthur to shower and dry himself so that he'd know what to do when his swimming classes started the following week. Though she was sure that there would be water collecting on the floor afterwards and that the wet towel would be left on his pillow, she had learned over the years to set a low pass mark for things, and in that way look upon today as an improvement on yesterday, and not as a subtraction from perfection. His boxers would be a little wet as he hadn't yet figured how to dry his body's awkward creases around that area, but no matter, in little ways he was growing in the general direction of independence. Even though he was a mere one dog year old, he had already been many different children. Back when he was about three or four, everything was about White Bus. Where's White Bus? Who's got White Bus? No sleep, no getting into the car, no leaving the house – anyone's house – until White Bus was found. He didn't even remember that now. Arthur's mind was like an Etch A Sketch where new images could only be formed by wiping out what was there before.

He lay on his bed tummy-wise and extended his left hand for Marie-Thérèse to do his grooming regime, starting with clipping the nails on fingers and toes, then cotton buds in his ears, followed by cream for the dry skin on his doughy biceps.

'Your muscles are getting big. I told you all those vegetables would pay off,' she said.

'Muscles are made from meat, not vegetables. And anyway, muscles are no good if you're fighting someone who has guns.'

'True. You've an answer for everything. Here, tell me a joke from your book, will you?'

'Right: What has fifty legs but can't walk?' asked Arthur.

'Erm... A walking stick shop?'

'Half a centipede.'

'Right, all done for today,' she said, leaning in for one of his dry kisses. He arranged his soft toys around him according to his own system, while she straightened the covers and tucked the excess into the gap at the wall.

'Arthur?'

'Yes?'

'Remember I said that there was a lovely house up where Nana lives?'

'The one with the big fridge that has an ice maker?'

'No, that's Nana's house – remember I said how we might be moving to a new house and that we'd be near the sea and everything?'

'Oh yeah. Not really.'

'I wanted to check with you whether you have any thoughts about it, or whether there's anything you'd like to have an Arthur-and-Mama chat about.'

'Like what?'

'Like are you happy about it?'

It was the question she had decided, tactically, not to ask. The question that would most likely gather together all his worries and hers. The question that would settle whether or not she was imposing on Arthur the same disrupted childhood she was still recovering from. If he said yes, that he was happy about it, then the decision was made; and if he said no, then he said no, and the temptation to scrap it all on his account would be unbearable, but they would move anyway because what other choice did she, or they, have? That was the way things went in her life of guilty decisions. Guilt. What was it? A way of torturing those who were already trying the hardest.

'I don't know,' said Arthur. 'I forgot about it.'

Arthur didn't live in the hypothetical. Either things were happening now, or had already happened. What might be had no reality. The future belonged to the imagination, something that children were trained to distinguish from real life.

She knelt there with his feet getting cold on her lap.

'Never mind,' she said. 'Five more minutes and then turn off the big light.'

'Can you leave the waves here?'

Marie-Thérèse brought the egg-shaped speaker into his room and left her phone with him.

'You can turn off the light if you want,' he said. 'Will you do my eyebrows?'

She started off the wave sounds and as they shushed on the window sill she stroked his eyebrows with her thumb, at first with the direction of the hair and then, too tempted to do otherwise, against it.

'Don't,' he whispered, smiling at her doing exactly what she always did. 'You'll give me forehead-ache.'

'Here – let me brush it back again.'

His eyes closed and she could feel his breath slowing on her wrist. Life should always be like that. Resting safely, with someone looking over you, attending to the little indulgences that loved people enjoy. There were times, she would admit, when for all her heroic independence, her sacred resilience, she would have liked to trust her weight to the love of another person like that. To fall backwards in absolute security. But she had only known doubting love. Love that needed to be weighed against what it cost. She was exhausted. Everything was so hard.

Downstairs, she picked up the clothes and shoes scattered about the place, feeling discouraged more than resentful. She had a restless heart. Alone, but in no mood for company, nothing appealed to her. As she sat down on the couch, on the sunken cushion where her dad usually sat, she rubbed the patch behind her ear. The tiredness she had stored in her body began to soak her muscles in a fatigue that felt like debt. Even her worries were tired, her problems presenting themselves with tidal repetition, beaching before they came to a clear point. At times like this she fantasised about getting sick. The luxury of conscience-free rest. Let the world run things for a while. Sleep during the day. Read a book – a book! The thought of it. When did that last happen? These were her fantasies now. Not about love or success or material comfort. Fantasies about respite from the relentlessness of the world.

The obvious answer to all this was sleep. Nobody ever regretted sleep. Yet there was part of her that rebelled against becoming one of those people who kept nothing of the day for themselves. Though her body longed for restorative rest, her *personality* – the part of her that used to say interesting things and make people laugh – kicked inside her somewhere. It also made her see the naked things that she could admit but not defend; the things she could never repeat in front of witnesses. Like maybe it wasn't always better to have people in your life. Maybe it wasn't always better to have children, or a relationship, or a family. It was a trick question of course. Loyalty meant pretending not to see certain things. There was a valve in some choices that allowed you in but never out; or if out, then never out and back to where you had been before. Relationships never truly ended, and even when people faded from you their effect was preserved somewhere in the particle physics of experience where everything is a compound made up of traces of everything else.

Marie-Thérèse could riff like that all night if she allowed herself. It was all part of the crusading honesty that characterised her world view and self-view. Nobody was spared. Regardless of whether she believed those thoughts, she could see they existed. It fascinated her how deep they could go, and how persuasive they were. Was that what depression amounted to? Seeing the merit in bad thoughts? Maybe they had a point.

She went to the kitchen and made a sandwich for her dad for when he came in from wherever he was. Her mother had taught her about the value of an act of love every day, and had lived it too. But Marie-Thérèse could do all that stuff and feel no pulse of love in it, purely the mechanics of making the other person happy because things were easier that way.

Her phone was charging in the kitchen on the countertop. When she checked it later that evening, a message would be waiting for her from Vincent, about how they really needed to talk.

# Chapter 22: Weeding

It was the weekend, and Panenka was helping Esther make something of her new house, an end-terrace rental with a balding lawn at the front and a square courtyard to the rear which was paved over and had deep, weedy borders. The rooms were painted in landlord magnolia and furnished with chino-coloured flat pack. Panenka noticed its clean, empty, art gallery feel. It held no clues about her.

'How come you picked this place? Wouldn't it have been better to take an apartment closer to town?' he asked

'Don't you like it?'

'It's nice. Lots of dead space though.'

'Space is the most expensive part of a property.'

Panenka walked around calling echoes and clapping to hear the reverberations. It was his first time being invited to her home and he had accepted the invitation innocently, though not without worrying that they were getting closer than was fair to her. He found it hard not to indulge the small, sweet madness of denial in accepting her into his life when so much else was slipping away.

'How do you want to do this? Split up or work in teams?' she asked.

She looked nice in her gardening clothes. A saggy hat and an old t-shirt that looked loved.

'Why don't we start in the garden together and then do indoor stuff if it rains,' he suggested.

Outside in the courtyard, Esther crouched down to weed and asked him to follow her around with the primary-coloured bedding plants in the hollows she left behind. They didn't have a spare trowel so Panenka used the scoop that came with the laundry powder. They could hear the breeze hissing through the trees in the gardens around them, though the courtyard was sheltered and still, like a room.

'I hear your football team is doing well,' she said. 'Everyone in the shop has been telling me.'

'So long as they don't lose their last game they'll be promoted back to the top division.'

'You going to go to it?'

'I haven't been in years.'

'Why don't you watch it here then?' she asked.

'I might not be great company during a Seneca match. And I've been trying hard not to show you my bad side.'

'It would do you good to watch it with the last calm person in town, and I can't not learn about this stuff. Besides, I'm curious about your bad side. We need to be visible to each other.'

She was right, of course; she always made true things sound simpler than they were.

'It might even make me feel better after embarrassing myself on the bridge the other night.'

'You're saying that to the man who cried over a haircut.'

'I hadn't planned to start into the whole Eugene drama, that's all. I had hoped to keep him locked away in the attic for a little longer. But I suppose I've always been a blurter.'

'You were brave about it, I thought. You're right to talk about these things. I wish I was more like you,' said Panenka.

'Do you not think we're alike?' she asked.

He twisted his mouth. 'I don't have your comfort with yourself. You can improvise; I can't do that. But you're a good influence on me. I'm not sure what sort of influence I am on you, though.'

'I feel... I feel like you're on my team. I haven't had someone like that in my life for a while.'

They were side by side as they talked, hunched over the beds they were digging, the air leafy and warm. The activity disguised the intimacy of it.

'I like that it's quiet,' she remarked after a while.

'Won't the quiet get to you – won't you be lonely here? There isn't much to do around this area. It's all old people.'

'I'm not scared of that. Loneliness is a torch: it can show you things about yourself. '

They were starting to run out of bedding plants so Panenka switched to collecting up the bits of weeds scattered around the paving and stuffing them into a heavy duty green plastic sack.

After a while, Esther stopped and balanced on her haunches, pushing back her gardening hat with the back of her glove. 'Can I ask you a question?' She blew something away from her face. 'I warn you that it's personal.'

'Personal about you or personal about me?'

'Both-ish.'

'Go on.'

'Do you know the way, between two people, there's wanting to but can't, wanting to but won't and then not wanting to?' she said.

'I do now.'

'Well, would it be a very bad thing – from your point of view – if I were the kind of person who wanted to but can't. But not because I don't want to. If that makes sense.'

Panenka was pressing a clump of nettles into the bag carefully and thought about his answer.

'When you first came into my life,' he said, 'I couldn't figure out what you were to me, or what I was supposed to be to you. But I like myself when I'm with you. You make me quiet inside.'

He stopped with the nettles and looked at her.

'I'm not going to drive a hard bargain, Esther.'

Esther had stopped working to listen to him.

'I hope you know, I didn't invite you over just to ask you that,' she said. 'It wasn't meant to sound like a trap or anything. But I felt I should gamble on trust and be honest – let go of the trapeze and hope you'd be there with another. I'm sorry things aren't different. I hope you're not disappointed. I do have a lot of room in my heart for you, you know that – it's just I can't do anything about it right now.'

She squinted up at him.

'Do you want to stop seeing me?' he asked.

'You're one of my favourite people, Joseph. I want to be fair to you. I'm giving you the chance to stop seeing *me* if you want.'

'And then what would I do?'

She smiled in a girlish way he hadn't seen before.

'I don't know... chase some football woman or something,' she smirked.

Panenka flicked some weed mud at her and her ridiculous suggestion, and the conversation surfed a bunch of unanswered questions.

After they had done their work, and before anything complicated happened, Panenka made his excuses and got ready to leave. Esther helped him put on his tracksuit top at the door, messing with the zip up and down, trying to make a tune out of it: 'That was meant to be The Entertainer – here: listen.'

She went to start it again but he held her fingers gently. He could see she was stalling.

'What is it?' he asked.

'Why can't a woman have a deep affinity with a man, though? Perhaps even love him, and he can love her, but it doesn't have to become romantic. Then it's okay if you love the person. You don't have to pretend you don't, or hide any subterfuge about being more than friends. Why not? Isn't there something missing if two people can't love each other safely that way? Like the way it's possible to love Paris without owning it, or the way we love music. Appreciative love. We need to find people like that, who cultivate what's good in us, and who can help draw out our poison. Otherwise, it's almost like if you don't want to fall in love, then you're on your own, that's *it*.' She did a karate chop. 'But why should we have to wait until we're happy before we can be loved? Before letting someone in? It's the hurt people who need love the most, who deserve it most, who understand it most.'

'So what are we to call this then?' he asked.

'Let's not name it. Once you name something, you have to define it: say what it is and isn't. Not to mention maintenance. All the relationships with names – parent, sister, husband, *lover* – come with maintenance. All that effort keeping it to what it's supposed to be. Shouldn't we allow ourselves at least one unnamed, undefined close relationship in our lives? A free-standing, wild-card arrangement. How about it, Joseph? How about you just try to make me happy, and I'll try and do the same for you?'

# Chapter 23: Baby Tooth

'Thanks Carla,' said Marie-Thérèse.

'No problem at all. It's been ages since I've had quality time with my favourite man in the world. We're going to get married when you grow up, aren't we Arthur?'

'I'm not sure. There might not be room in my motorhome,' said Arthur.

'A motorhome! I love motorhomes. I'd be like a real princess in one of those.' Carla leaned in to whisper: 'Arthur – I can't remember, but I thought I saw a packet of crisps in the corner cupboard in the kitchen. Would you mind checking for me?'

Arthur shot past her.

*'Bye Arthur,'* called Marie-Thérèse to the empty space he left behind. *'Don't overdo the treats and be good for Carla. I'll pick you up in a little while.'*

'He'll be fine. I'll fill him full of bribes until he tells me what you say about me behind my back.'

'All praise Carla, believe me. I'm not looking forward to this. Could you go for me?'

'Vincent is your husband. It's in the marriage contract: lots of big talks.'

'Are you going to watch the match?'

'I'll put it on, but I'll let Arthur watch a movie if he gets bored. Are you going to watch it with Vincent?'

'I had honestly forgotten that it was on tonight when we arranged to meet. It was the one evening we were both free, but I'm sure he thinks I'm testing him. I'd better go. Thanks again.'

Driving over to Vincent's apartment, Marie-Thérèse felt a little low but composed. By that point her relationship with Vincent was like a baby tooth wobbling with inevitability but which wouldn't quite fall out by itself. She expected he would plan and script his case for staying together, but she trusted her own clarity. For her, the conversation was already over; there was no bargain to be had. The relationship had taught her all about the dangers of falling deeply into someone else's life and drowning there. It was a question of allowing him the space to say whatever he had to say, clumsy or cinematic, she didn't mind.

'Come on in,' he said.

He smelled of aftershave, though not one she recognised. She used to buy him the same designer brand every Christmas, the one he had worn on their wedding day; she liked smelling it around his collarbone as they lay together. The smell that said he was hers. When was the last bottle she had bought him – two, maybe three years before? They had stopped buying presents altogether long before they broke up. A sign that they were running out of love and all its attention to details.

'I'm not long out of the shower. I was a bit delayed in work.'

'Because of the match?' she asked.

'No, it would have been slow tonight. We don't even have a TV for customers yet so we would have been the quietest place in town.'

'Am I making you miss it?'

'Not at all. Seneca can handle things without me, I'm sure. It would take a freakish set of results for them not to go up. I'm glad we're finally getting to talk though. It's overdue don't you think? Would you like a drink? Wine, coffee?'

'I'll have some water. Tap water's fine.'

'Sure? I have soda water. I run a café-bar. I can at least offer you something interesting.'

'Whatever. You decide.'

Vincent brought her a drink – ginger beer, with ice and a slice of lemon. She regretted having sat on the couch. Now he would either have to sit right up beside her or else make a point of sitting on the armchair, three or four symbolic feet away. Vincent, uncomplicated Vincent, sat down on the couch.

'You first,' he said.

'To be honest I don't have a lot to say. Basically, I was planning to move to a new place once I can get the transfer at work finalised, but I'll need to stay on for another month or two, so I still have a bit of time to make arrangements. Everything needs to be sorted for the new school year in September, but that might be expecting too much. My mother said she knows the Principal and can help get Arthur a place, but if we miss September it all becomes complicated. I'm not sure what else to add?'

Vincent took a drink from his bottle of beer and wiped his mouth with his wrist.

'Don't I feature at all in your plans?' he asked meaningfully.

'Vincent, look, I think we're probably overdue a whole bunch of conversations. Which one are we having tonight?'

'I'm not looking to fight you, Marie-Thérèse.'

'You never fight. You exasperate. That's your style. You're never the aggressor, but you're still trying to get your own way. Still pushing me.'

'Marie-Thérèse, I love you. You're my wife and Arthur is my son. Don't I have some standing in all this? Can't I question how you're hollowing out our family? I've never hurt you or done anything to disrespect or mistreat you. What's with all this coldness? Ten and a half years we've been together—'

'That's right. Don't forget the half year.'

'—and after all that, you want to turn it off like a machine. This past year has been difficult for me but I've always tried to do the right thing. What else do I need to do? You need to tell me, Marie-Thérèse, because we can't solve this separately.'

Marie-Thérèse had finished her ginger beer. There were many things she could say and many ways she could say them.

'Vincent, I've never asked anything of you that you shouldn't already expect of yourself. You think that I'm looking for you to pull some sword from a stone. Even though you're a grown man you like to think that life is about someone turning around and telling you that you've done the right thing, and if somebody tells you that, if *I* tell you that, well then, under the rules, bad things can't happen. But that's not what's going on here at all. What's going on is that I'm telling you, and have been telling you for the past year, that we can't be together anymore. You don't have to have done something wrong for me to feel that way. It's not a punishment, and there's no blame in what I'm saying to you. This is happening because sometimes relationships don't last. That's all. It's possible to fail honestly.'

She walked across the room and helped herself to a drink from the fridge, a territorial assertion.

'You think we've failed?' he said, pivoting so that his point could follow her as she passed him. 'Maybe we need to try harder. We shouldn't give up unless we're sure, we're really sure. It's too important. Every relationship gets tested, every *family* gets tested. Sure, you have doubts, that's natural. But you can't build a future around doubts – don't overlook the certainties you already have.'

She sat back down with her drink – on the other chair this time – and spoke calmly. 'I don't want to do this with big heavy statements that, once we say them, will stay between us always.'

'Please don't speak in code, Marie-Thérèse.'

'Vincent,' she said, turning to face him, 'I don't love you any more. I did once, with all my heart, but it has faded. It faded all by itself. It wasn't anything you or I did, it's just that it was a young love. A love that was magic when everything was simple, when life was all ahead of us, but it didn't have the depth to sustain us when our world became more complicated. It was a love that couldn't feed us. Couldn't feed me.'

'You're oversimplifying to make yourself feel better.'

'No, Vincent! Our love wore off a long time ago. I could feel it happening and I didn't know what it was. I thought I was starting to hate you. Every word you said irritated me. I could find fault in everything you did. And then, there was this one day when we were in the park and I looked at you properly and you were smiling with Arthur and I came to a realisation: "This is a good man. A nice person. There's nothing wrong with him. I simply don't love him anymore." I could feel my body and my heart and everything unclench once I understood that. And you are, Vincent. A decent person and a great father to Arthur. I'm lucky that my son has such a loving dad. But you and I are over. I need you to accept that. If you do, we can be great parents, but if you don't, we're going to keep having this sort of conversation and, speaking for myself, I'm not sure how many more big talks I have left in me.'

Vincent was staring off into the room as though her words had arranged themselves there. She moved to the couch and touched his hand but he didn't respond. She had broken his heart. She knew that.

'Vincent?'

He was gathering himself, or maybe reassembling himself.

'I'm not trying to make you do anything you don't want to do,' he said calmly. 'I suppose what you're telling me is that I don't excite you or inspire you anymore, assuming I ever did. That's a hard thing to hear, but I'm not trying to win an argument. The idea of a victory at your expense is alien to me. Your loss is my loss.'

'Look, I'm sorry Vincent—'

'Please,' he said, resisting her comfort. 'Allow me a little dignity. I should at least be allowed to express myself. It must hardly matter to you now, but it matters to me.'

She sat back into the couch. They were two separate people now.

'In spite of what you say, I still love you,' he said. 'For me, love is not something I can take up and put down. Love is not a decision. I accept what you say about your feelings and I'll respect that, but it's not up to me whether I continue loving you or not.'

'Vincent, you need to understand that I watched my parents persist in a marriage that should have ended years before it did. Prolonging these things is not a way to hold on to love: it won't defy gravity.'

'I'm not asking you to do that. But I'm not your father and you're not your mother. We had our own chance to be happy and it was ours alone. Only you can know if you're doing this to escape what happened to your parents, but I can tell you this, as someone who wishes only good things for you: trying not to repeat someone else's history is a wasteful way to live.'

An unfinished quiet hung between them like a cordon of sensitivity; the pressure to say dangerous things was palpable, as was the sense that there would be no other opportunity to say them.

'You know, this is probably the longest conversation we have had in the year we've been apart,' she said. 'In several years, maybe. When we met, you were the first person, perhaps the only person, interested enough to pay attention to my way of being in the world, to map me and formulate theories about who I was and how I was. Even when you were wrong about me – perhaps especially when you were wrong – those theories always made me feel like I mattered to someone, and they provoked me to define myself, to make my defence and to draw myself in clearer, unbroken lines.

'You've always been and I hope it's still possible for you to be an important person in my life. But not as a husband, Vincent. All that's happened is that we've found out each other's limits, and learned something about our own limits. That much is rare between any two people. Failure is not waste. But maybe I would have found it easier to appreciate you if my happiness didn't depend on you so much.'

It was meant as a healing tribute of sorts, to salve what she was sundering. Despite what he had said, it was she who saw no value in winning at his expense.

'What if,' he said, 'What if I moved out of this place and you and Arthur took it instead?'

'What would you do?'

'I'd find somewhere. Just promise me you won't take Arthur away.'

'Okay, Vincent. Okay.'

# Chapter 24: Violent fireworks

By the time Panenka arrived home from work, Marie-Thérèse had already left to meet Vincent for their summit. He had missed a text from her reminding him that she would be out and that Arthur was being minded at Carla's. Her life, as ever, meant having a million and one things to think about. There was also a text from Esther: Bring wine!

Esther had invited him to watch the match at her house over a good-luck dinner, for which she was taking the trouble to unpack whatever was in the box marked KITCHEN STUFF (PROBABLY). He was being unfair to her, he knew that. At some point he would have to tell her the truth about things and shed the circumspection that had started to weigh on him like the lie it was, but his commitment to do something about it had already been subject to several deferrals. He wasn't sure whether he needed more time to make sense of it himself, or just wasn't ready to lose her.

Panenka had worked through his lunch break to finish early, using energy on credit, and his body now reminded him that it was owed a skipped meal. Stiff around the shoulders and with his temples pulsing from over-concentration, he stood with the fridge door open, looking for inspiration, but only finding Arthur's lunch snacks for school: cheese dips with little breadsticks, which would have to do. He ate standing up, his balance fighting a melting fatigue.

Upstairs he took off his work clothes, catching the stale must of his top as he peeled it over his head, and ran the shower. Under the water, his hands made his usual figure eight shapes around his body, rubbing across his chest and under his oxters, the heat inducing a bed-like feeling in him, uterine and comforting. He had a footballer's habit of quick showers and so, with Esther and Seneca waiting, he shut off the water and stood amidst the steam, sweating a little as he dried himself off.

When it came, it struck like a boot to the head. First, there was a single flash of pain from within, and then, launched in succession, a second and a third. Violent fireworks. Instinctively, he covered his head as if the assault had come from outside him. On his knees, he pressed his cheek with panicked futility against the bath side and then his forehead against the slippery floor tiles, his body curling like a prawn. The pain was without sound, colour or shape; an edgeless, unreasonable assailant. Words and thoughts abandoned him like cowards. All that remained was the pressure insisting on itself. Just Panenka and the Iron Mask.

# Chapter 25: Seneca's last match

It was after ten when Marie-Thérèse arrived to pick up Arthur.

'Apologies, Carla. I didn't realise the time. I think I underestimated how much there was to unpick with Vincent.'

'How'd it go?'

'I'm exhausted. Maybe we should have discussed all this a long time ago. But it was hard. Hard for us both.'

'You done good. Arthur was a sweetheart. He helped me organise all my jewellery and everything. He's really into bits and pieces isn't he? Loves rooting around. He's tired though. *Arthur, your mother's here*,' she called into the back.

Arthur arrived at the door sucking one end of a jelly snake, as though it were a penny whistle he was playing.

'Look – I got this,' he said holding up his wrist to show that he was wearing Carla's old white Swatch. 'All it needs is a battery.'

'What do you say to Carla?'

'Thanks,' he said.

Carla bent down to kiss him, but he kissed her arm instead.

'He's not into wet kisses,' explained Marie-Thérèse.

Arthur fell asleep in the car on the way home. The traffic had cleared after the match, but the streets were full of people running around with Seneca flags draped over their shoulders and cars driving around with topless men leaning out of the windows, pressing on horns in celebration at their team's 4-1 home win and a return to the top division for the first time in twenty-five years. The Seneca victory held nothing for Marie-Thérèse. No interest, no resolution. It was just another thing in the world.

When she went to lift Arthur out of his car seat, he was holding the jelly snake she had forgotten to take from him. His face was a portrait of open-mouthed innocence. She peeled the snake from his fingers and cleaned his hand and lips with wipes before moving him. He stirred as she struggled to open the door single-handed.

'Can I press the alarm?'

'Go ahead,' she said, disappointed at him waking up, especially if the short nap had taken the edge off his sleepiness. Tonight was not a night where she wanted to spend hours settling down a sugared-up child. All she wanted was to get his teeth brushed and for him to get back to sleep, so she could open the bottle of white wine that stood waiting in the fridge door, finish off the slab of dark chocolate she had been resisting all week, and have a little cry in front of a bad movie.

'Go on upstairs and hop into your jammies Arthur – they're under your pillow.'

'Can I say goodnight to Pop?'

'I'd say he's gone out, but you can check.'

Marie-Thérèse went back out to the car to bring in Arthur's bag of stuff, and to wipe away the gooey mess she expected to find on the car seat. The air around her was cool and peaceful as she closed her eyes and let the breeze soothe her cheeks. She was now officially independent. Her relationship with Vincent had been severed that night. Ten years of her life unloaded: a terminal moraine of memories, intimacies, doubts and details. She had decided long ago that this was how it had to be but it was only now that the full reality spread through her and the first ripples of grief began to form.

And she had agreed to stay. It was a decision on instinct, like grabbing the arm of a falling child. Her mother was wrong. The problem was not where she lived, but who she loved. The answer didn't need to be found so much as recognised, and it was only when it came to her that she realised how long she had been carrying it.

'*Mama! Mama!*' shouted Arthur from inside, his voice carrying with panic from the upstairs landing.

Marie-Thérèse snapped around and launched herself through the front door and up the stairs, abandoning her bags in the hall.

'Arthur! Arthur! Are you all right? What happened?'

Arthur was in tears at the top of the stairs and immediately sank into Marie-Thérèse's breast, gripping her sides in a desperate embrace.

'What is it, buddy? I'm here, what is it?' she asked, holding his face with both hands and looking for signs of damage – a cut, a bump – quickly scanning his body, frisking him with an instinctive urgency. 'Are you hurt, Arthur? Please tell me.'

'Pop is dead! He's on the floor! He's on the floor!' he bawled.

Marie-Thérèse ran to the bathroom, where her father lay unconscious on the tiles with a towel around his waist. He was pale and she couldn't tell if he was breathing. What was she supposed to do? She tried his wrist for a pulse but couldn't tell if she felt one or was feeling her own racing heart. She put her hand in front of his mouth. There was a breath. Good, okay, there was a breath.

'Dad, Dad! Can you hear me? Can you hear me, Dad?'

She turned on the tap and cupped some cold water to throw on his face. He winced at it and groaned.

'Dad, Dad! It's Marie-Thérèse. Can you hear me? Say something!'

'I can hear you,' he said groggily. 'I can hear you.'

'Oh God. Oh, dear Lord, thank you, thank you,' said Marie-Thérèse crying, everything releasing at once and bursting through her.

'Arthur, he's awake,' she called, sobbing. 'He's awake. Pop is awake.'

Arthur came as far as the doorway before throwing himself around Panenka.

'Silly Pop, falling asleep in the bathroom,' said Panenka, his eyes becoming teary as he looked at the crumpled distress on his daughter's beautiful face. He rubbed her cheek. 'I'm okay, chicken, I promise.'

It took a while to settle Arthur, who lay awake and was quiet for a long time. Processing. Once he was asleep, Panenka arranged the soft toys the way he liked them: Piglet and Spiderman inside the sheets, and Snakey, the draft excluder, on the pillow above his head.

Panenka sat up in his own bed with a honey and lemon drink on his lap and a pillow behind his back, as Marie-Thérèse sat sideways-on, listening to his account of the Iron Mask and what he had been going through over the previous months. She simply listened and fidgeted with Arthur's plush Incredible Hulk, fastening and unfastening the Velcro on his purple trousers.

'Shouldn't we take you to the hospital?'

'I don't think so. Realistically, they've already said there's nothing that can be done.'

'So... how long are we talking about?' she asked.

'They're not sure. Months, maybe longer. It could stabilise for a time, they said, or get worse. The only thing they were sure of was that it wouldn't get better.'

He addressed the answer to his mug as his thumbs rubbed along its rim.

'But it's the first time this has happened during the day isn't it? It sounds like it's shifting. Are you not worried? I certainly am.'

'Who knows? I was a bit dizzy when I came in, but I was stupid not eating and I probably overdid things, brought it on myself. Oh, shit! Shit! Shit! Shit!'

'Oh my God, is it coming back?' asked Marie-Thérèse in a panic. 'Tell me what to do, quickly – do I need to ring an ambulance?'

'Esther! Poor Esther will be wondering what happened. Can you run down and get my phone for me? It's in the kitchen.'

'Oh Jesus Christ, you scared me. Don't do that. Who's Esther?'

'Please – could you get it for me? It's important.'

Marie-Thérèse brought the phone up. There were missed calls, and a couple of texts. The first one said 'You on your way?' The last one in the series said '?'

Panenka tried ringing but Esther's phone was switched off. He sent her a message apologising and asking her to call him, but not to worry.

'Shit!' he repeated, 'Shit!'

'Who's Esther?' asked Marie-Thérèse again.

'She's my friend.'

'Friend, or girlfriend?'

'Friend. She's more than a friend actually. More than a girlfriend, too.'

'I don't understand. Are you seeing each other?'

'It's a different type of thing.'

'Are you having an affair? Is she married?'

'No, no, it's not like that. It's, it's hard to explain.'

Marie-Thérèse looked straight at her dad with sniper eyes.

'What about our relationship? Are we something different too?' she asked.

'You're my daughter – I love you. Of course I do. How can you even ask that?'

Marie-Thérèse threw the plush Hulk at him.

'Oh, stop it! You have a serious condition and a whole new relationship and you don't even tell me? What am I? Who am I to you? Some minor character in your life? I bet this Esther knows about me and all about the headaches. Some woman you're texting. A special relationship all right. Meanwhile, your dumb family walks around knowing nothing about you. Who are you? Tell me. Seriously, I'd love to know. For once, I'd love to have a picture of who my dad is. One with *all* the details: the details I know about *and* the ones I'm ignorant of. I've invested in you, you stupid bastard. I've invested my*self* in you. I've invested Arthur's life in you. Mother told me to be careful. Not to assume that you would allow me to slot into your world. I told her – like the big idiot I am – I told her that it was my decision. That I deserved to build my own relationship with you. That I deserved a fresh start of my own. You secretive shit!'

'Marie-Thérèse, please, I don't think I can do this now. I've had a rough evening and I promise I'll explain when I'm better. It's not the way you describe it at all.'

'How could it be? It would be a miracle if I could describe anything about how your life works. After all, I'm only your daughter. The daughter who lives with you and who shares her life with you. It's all one way, though. You don't trust me to know anything. Things are set up so I will always misunderstand you. That's the way you like it. You don't want to be understood. You want to be mysterious. But you can't have it that way. I'm either fully in or fully out.'

Arthur began to stir in the room next door. They froze for a few moments until he settled.

'I'm sorry, Marie-Thérèse,' he said, his voice lowered. 'I really am. I'm not good at this, I know. I need to learn. I didn't tell you the truth about the headaches because you've done so much for me and I thought you deserved better than to become burdened with all that. You're making your plans to move to your new job and a new place and to start a fresh page, and I didn't want to say anything to change your mind for my sake. I wanted our relationship to be a happy and supportive one. I thought you'd have left by now and you wouldn't have to deal with any of this.'

'But you don't understand. That's exactly my problem. I'm the person you *should* be coming to about this. If you truly loved me you would let me in on these things. You'd come to me and we'd have no secrets from each other.'

Marie-Thérèse's shoulders dropped.

'Oh my God,' she said. 'After all this time, this is it.'

'What? What is it?'

'This is finally it. I've just realised that I have walked into the conversation I've both wanted and avoided for twenty-odd years,' she said.

'Maybe we've been resisting it for too long,' he said. 'Perhaps we both needed to be pushed to a point where we can't have any other conversation. If we want to move on, that is.'

Marie-Thérèse leaned over and took the Hulk back into her lap.

'When you were born,' he began, 'your mother and I had a shared plan that we were going to be this happy little family who had no money worries and who spent loads of time together, living in each other's pockets. And then the game against Olympik happened and my life sort of snapped. And after that I recoiled away from everyone, including you and your mother. Lauren did everything to hold us together, to rescue us. She wanted us to move away and shed the ridiculous overreaction. But I couldn't do it. I couldn't stay but I couldn't leave. I took the worst option of all: I put you both through a state of living abandonment. I disappeared into myself and lived in exile in my own town. I can't account for the years, except to say that I wasted them. I think I was in this in-between state where I needed to be surrounded by love but I couldn't let it touch me.'

He reached out to stroke her fingers. Outside, young men were chanting loudly, taking over the streets.

'But that's all about you,' she said. 'What about me?'

She lifted her hand out from under his.

'You know, in the first few weeks and months after everything fell to pieces, you saved me,' he said. 'You were three at the time and you and I created our own world. We had many, many tea parties with your teddies. You sat on my lap and I read you all your books over and over. I'll never forget them. You were able to read before you went to school – did you know that?'

'I have my mother's brains,' she said.

'I used to bring down my old stereo and play you all those songs about the woman who swallowed a fly, Tubby the Tuba, the Monster Mash. You were a blessing; always have been. When you started preschool that September I missed you. I think those long mornings alone, when your mother was at work and you were gone, was when I started to change. I felt lovesick not having your soft body to hold. You were tiny but your absence was as big as a whale. It sounds stupid but I was almost jealous that you were happy in a new routine that didn't include me. I wasn't well then. It became too much: missing you painfully when you were gone during those long mornings, and then being unable to adjust to having you. Something shifted and the pressure leaked into our house.'

He checked her face to see if he should go on. Whether he was making things worse. Her fingers picked at the Hulk's hair as she listened.

'That first summer,' he continued, 'when I could pretend there was no outside, was beautiful. But once the world came in between us, I couldn't reach you anymore. The contrast was too sharp. That began a long, slow process. Once you stop believing in yourself, it's hard not to see yourself as anything but a problem for others. I'm not sure if that's an answer to anything for you – is it?'

Marie-Thérèse had listened quietly. She had never heard the part about their time together, but the rest – the rest was what she had lived.

'I think, in some ways, I always thought I was more grown up than I was,' she said, her voice a little dry. 'For too many years you were this absent presence in my life. You were like a dangerous sun: even at a distance you could still burn me. I wanted you so badly and yet there was no stability to you. You were close enough to exist, but never close enough to hold onto. I think it left me with a feeling that my life was never entirely mine. All those years I kept this place open for you.' She pressed her hand against her chest. 'I would have denied it at the time – would have said that you didn't deserve it – but as Vincent, of all people, reminded me earlier this evening: you can't decide not to love someone.'

She pushed a lose strand of hair behind her left ear, rubbing the patch there briefly as she did so.

'Who knows how I tried to fill or disguise that space inside me – or how I kept people at a distance so that *they* wouldn't fill it instead. But I've had enough of psychology. People are always telling me what I'm like. Why is that?' she asked, turning towards him. 'I suppose everyone knows my story, so I've probably always battled against that. Others know more about me than I know about them; and I have to fight to make them accept *my* version of myself. To them, every emotional move I make is me acting out this folksy karma to do with a stupid football match. God, no wonder people think I'm so serious. No wonder *I* think I'm so serious.'

Marie-Thérèse stood up and lifted her keys and purse from where she had thrown them on the bedside table. She walked over to the open window and pulled it closed, shutting out the town's happiness. As she passed his bed on the way out of the room, she stopped to kiss her fingers and touch them to his lips.

In the doorway, she paused, lifting her eyes upwards as she listened out for signs of movement from Arthur.

'You know,' she said, her voice lowered, 'as I got older I noticed that you needed me more than I needed you. And, in a way, part of me wanted to deny you. The prospect of payback was tempting. I've grown up carrying this grieving child inside me and I was angry at you on her behalf. If I had to, I could set out all my reasons for having you back in my life, but truthfully, I don't know what I'm doing. Sometimes I want to take on the whole world and then there are other times ... when all I want is for the world to take care of me.'

Marie-Thérèse blinked to let the tears fall in ribbons down her rounded cheeks.

'And now all this,' she said. 'And now all this.'

# Chapter 26: Toasting Teddy

It was the last day of Teddy's placement. He had worked the maximum number of hours permitted under the government scheme, and with business too slow for Vincent to offer him a job, never mind a career, the welfare office had decided to enrol him on a six-week barista course instead. Vincent had come down to the café-bar early to set the place up, but by the time he arrived Teddy had already mopped the floor, checked the float for the till, restocked the fridges, emptied the dishwasher, vacuumed the mats and changed the soap and towels in the bathroom.

'We're going to miss you, Teddy. You've fitted in here nicely. I hope we can count on you as a customer,' said Vincent. 'You know I'd love to keep you on, don't you? But with the business being the way it is and everything...'

'Yeah, I understand. I've enjoyed it. If ever you're looking for someone though, keep me in mind won't you?'

'Absolutely. And if you ever need a reference ...'

There was an awkward pause, which was broken by Vincent offering an even more awkward handshake.

'The match was amazing wasn't it?' said Teddy, shifting gears. 'Now that's one night the town is not going to forget. Such an incredible buzz around the place. I'd say you had a bad headache this morning. Worth it though.'

'The kind of night you remember all right,' said Vincent.

For all the excitement about Seneca, the town was quiet that day. A spontaneous and unofficial public holiday had broken out, with many businesses closed or opening late, their staff calling in sick or looking to take the day off, only to find that their managers had already had the same idea. It was an outbreak of irresponsibility that would have been difficult to explain to outsiders. Yes, it was a celebration of rare sporting success, but it was also something more. The people of the town spoke in terms of a spell being broken and the lifting of a curse, language that reflected both their elation and their dogged superstition. The club had a new reference point now in which Cesar Fontaine and Panenka did not feature. There were new names to remember and Seneca, which had perhaps been guilty of using its tradition as an excuse for looking backwards, now had a generation of supporters who were tired of its folklore and instead sought new stories that belonged to their own time.

For Vincent, it was also a new start. He had slept little during the night, lying with his window open as the car horns sounded and drunken fans ran through the streets singing the full repertoire of chants he knew too well. He recounted to himself what he had gained and lost in his conversation with Marie-Thérèse. Like Seneca, he too needed to look ahead and make what he could of what he still held. It had been a lonely night, and he expected there would be many more of those, but he took solace in knowing that he hadn't lost Arthur and that while Marie-Thérèse was no longer his wife, he could finally accept that he had deserved her for all those years they had been together. He was glad to see his regulars as they arrived. It was a rare opportunity to view his own café-bar through their eyes: as a place of unencumbered friendship during uncertain times.

'Playing football, and in fact most exertive sport, is strictly for young people,' began BABA. 'Beyond a certain age it's unseemly to sweat in public on purpose.' His return a few days previously had been welcomed but not remarked upon. As BABA himself had often pointed out, it was not always best to talk about things.

'Tell us, how should men of our generation stay healthy then?' asked Anthony, noticeably invigorated by the return of his friend and rival.

'Swimming,' replied BABA. 'It's a dignified and gentlemanly way to exercise. The closest a man can get to flying.'

'You must be joking,' said Anthony. 'You have to parade around in your underwear in front of strangers. And it is *filthy*. I wouldn't touch Caesar's Palace swimming pool unless I was in a submarine.'

'I think he has a point,' said Vincent. 'Some people refer to the swimming pool as "The Baths" and I suspect they still use it as a form of public bath. You're supposed to shower before swimming, but, honestly, how many follow the rules?'

'Public bath is the least of it,' added Anthony. 'Some use it as a public toilet.'

'That's why they add chlorine,' pointed out Teddy. 'They don't trust people.'

Panenka hadn't been able to join them, and the others attributed his absence to the complicated emotions they supposed he must have been feeling following the Seneca result.

After they had toasted Teddy several times over, including a round of crème de menthes bought by BABA, the evening unwound. Teddy was picked up by his girlfriend, a stunner who led them to concede collectively that they had underestimated the young man.

Anthony smoked as he walked up the street with BABA.

'Wait: I need to nip down here,' said BABA as he unbuckled himself and stepped into an alley.

'Why didn't you go back in Vincent's? You think it's unseemly to sweat in public but not to piss in public?'

'What a pointless question – my bladder is not going to change its mind. Hey – don't stare at me! I'm relying on you as a lookout.'

'If you were that shy you wouldn't be undressing outdoors – you're a closet exhibitionist, if that's not an oxymoron.'

'It is. And don't pretend you've never done it.'

'I refute that. I only ever urinate in three places: work, home and hotels,' replied Anthony.

'Refute means disprove, not rebut. Anyway, surely you must go at Vincent's sometimes?'

'Not if I can avoid it. That toilet alone is enough of an explanation for why there are no female customers.'

BABA stepped out of the alley rubbing his fingertips together. Instinctively, they walked in the middle of the street where the light was better, the streetlamps on either side having blown bulbs here and there.

'I thought you had given those up?' said BABA about Anthony's smoking.

'I had.'

'Aren't you asthmatic?'

'I am,' said Anthony, exhaling through his nostrils. 'But it occupies me.'

BABA watched the smoke cling to the air then disperse.

'How are things at home?' he asked.

'Same,' said Anthony. 'So very the same.'

Their shadows moved across the road in front of them as they walked.

'What are you going to do – I mean, what *can* you do?' asked BABA, sincerely.

Anthony allowed a few thoughtful beats before answering.

'I'll wait,' he said. 'Sometimes when you love someone that's what you do. You wait for them.'

They continued together until the road split the way home for each of them. There the two men stood wordlessly, as BABA kept Anthony company so that he wouldn't have to smoke his sorrow alone.

# Chapter 27: Barbershop Duet

Marie-Thérèse leaned over the bridge, peeling an orange she had stolen from work and looking out over the dehydrated canal, a thread of sorry water running across its bed. She had given herself one orange's worth of thinking time before deciding what to do, and spat pips at a bent bicycle wheel that protruded archeologically from the mud below. It had been easy to scout out where the barber's was, recalling her dad saying that it was on the cathedral side of town near Luca the Gossip's shop. But as she watched Esther from the opposite side of the street the words she had come to say suddenly felt like gum chewed to tastelessness in her mouth. She was different to how Marie-Thérèse had imagined her: fortyish – no scandalous age gap; tastefully dressed, ladylike even; at ease in herself; full of demonstrative hand gestures that pulled invisible strings on the people she was talking to. It was uncomfortable for Marie-Thérèse to admit Esther's own reality, free of reference points to her dad. So there she stood, with an empty canal and a palm full of orange peelings in place of the inspiration she had been counting on.

Esther flashed Marie-Thérèse a distracted smile when she walked in. She was busy trimming the beard of an older man who was in the middle of telling an anecdote about himself, something to do with an unresolved grievance. There was a warmth to Esther, she could see that, her smiles and interjections providing affirmation to the men she had to listen to all day, making them feel interesting. As Marie-Thérèse watched her in the mirror she thought she could detect in Esther's generous, reassuring face, a look around the eyes, a private story that would have escaped her notice had she not seen it so often in her dad.

By the time Esther swivelled the chair around and offered it to her, the shop had emptied and the two of them were alone together.

'Actually, I didn't come here for a haircut,' said Marie-Thérèse.

'Oh?'

'I'm... I'm Panenka's daughter,' she said, pushing the words out against the will of her nerves.

'Who?'

'My name is Marie-Thérèse.'

'Oh, I see. Nice to meet you finally. And I suppose you know who I am.'

'Yes. Well, I know a little bit. I only found out about you very recently. Can we talk for a minute?'

'I'm not sure there's—'

'Please. It won't take long. I appreciate you're busy. He doesn't know I'm here. I didn't tell him.'

Esther walked over to the door and pulled down the blind. She took a seat on one of the barber chairs and offered Marie-Thérèse the other.

'Your dad has told me all about what a wonderful person you are. He's very proud of you.'

'I promise I'm not trying to interfere. But he's been like a wet mop since the other night. I think he misses you.'

'I know the feeling. I missed him.'

'If I can explain—'

Esther raised her palm pre-emptively.

'I think he should make his own explanations, Marie-Thérèse. Look, I don't mean to be rude but please don't take me for someone who's angry or sulking. I'm an adult. I don't want to be made to feel unreasonable when I'm entitled to feel hurt.'

'Esther,' said Marie-Thérèse. 'I was the one who found him.'

'What are you saying?'

'I found him unconscious on the bathroom floor. I thought he was dead.'

'What?'

'Actually, it was my son who found him. My dad has this... it's a condition. He gets these bad headaches that he says are like an iron mask on his face, like a clamp. They usually happen at night, but when he was getting ready to see you, they started coming on in a way that was stronger than ever before. He blacked out and was lucky he didn't hit his head and do worse damage. There was no way for him to let you know. He's lucky to be alive.'

'Oh dear God, I had no idea. He never mentioned anything. How is he?'

'He's fine. Or, at least the headaches haven't come back. Wait a minute, what am I saying, he's not fine. He will *tell* you he's fine but he's not. My dad is not a straightforward man – you might have figured that out already. He's already been through all the appointments and apparently there's nothing more they can do for him. He's known this for weeks but I've only just found out.'

'I don't know what to say. I simply had no idea. Is it a brain tumour or something? Will he need surgery?'

'He's past that stage. I'm trying to get him to open up about it all, but it's hard for him. I think he's more worried about everyone else – if he could deal with it alone, he would. So now you know. I'm not trying to change your mind about anything. Your relationship is your own business.'

'I wish I could say that I feel better now that you've told me, but it all sounds terrible. Where is he now?'

'He's at home with Arthur – that's my son.'

'I know who Arthur is,' said Esther, her face softening. 'I'd like to see your dad if that's possible.'

'Of course.'

Esther stood up and brushed off the loose hairs that had stuck to her trousers.

'How is your work situation?' she asked. 'Your dad told me you've a new job. A promotion, is that right? Congratulations.'

'I thought I was going to be good at it, but I'm starting to wonder if I'm a fake. And it's lonely being the person that everyone brings their problems to, don't you think?'

'It can be.'

'I had the chance to move to a different branch, but I've changed my mind. They've agreed to let me stay, but I think they view me differently now. I've turned into the woman who puts her family first. I've killed the mythical version of me they preferred. How do you do it – running your own business?'

'I took this on by accident, if I'm honest, a couple of months ago. I'm not even sure I'm the business type, but I think it's the people who doubt themselves that work out better. It makes you try your best; it makes you want to learn.'

'Aren't you afraid of failing? Letting everyone down?'

Esther thought about it.

'Maybe it's important that other people learn how to handle disappointment.'

She sorted the register cash into bags as Marie-Thérèse swept up the hair and helped to tidy things away. She had that instinctive retail touch for putting things in order.

'When you came in,' said Esther, 'I thought to myself "Now, what does she want done?" I guessed you were looking to have it all shaved off. We get a few women in here, but it's usually older women on a budget who wear their hair short anyway. The young women we get tend to be the "Shave it all off" type. They want to make a statement. But you didn't have that look about you.'

'I couldn't do that. I'd be too embarrassed.'

'Oh, but you've a lovely heart-shaped face. It might suit you.'

'What about this though?' she said, lifting the hair behind her left ear where the bald patch had grown a little bigger since Carla had last measured it.

'Does it bother you?' asked Esther.

'Not if nobody finds out about it. Do you know of any remedies? Doctors and pharmacists aren't much help.'

'Unfortunately, I think it might be one of those things you have to live with.'

Esther asked Marie-Thérèse to hold the door while she slipped into the back and punched in the alarm code, before dashing across the barbershop floor in mock panic. She locked the shutters and they walked down the street, waving across to Luca the Gossip who watched them from the front door of his shop. He was smoking a thin cigar and wearing a Marlboro apron, his free hand tucked into the front pocket of it.

'How do you find the neighbours?' asked Marie-Thérèse.

'Oh, they're not the worst. Luca told me he cuts his own hair, so I told him I didn't smoke, and that seemed to move us along. Do you know him?'

'Sort of. Not really. He knows my dad.'

'By the way,' said Esther, as they waited to cross the road. 'Why did you call him Panenka?'

# Chapter 28: Proverbs

'"When the poor man's buffalo calves, everyone runs with his pail for milk,"' read Panenka.

'What's that mean?' asked Arthur, who was lying supine on the couch with his head on his grandfather's lap.

'I think it means that poor people are more generous, or maybe that when they have good luck – which wouldn't be that often – they share it.'

'What about rich people? I don't think it's fair to make a rule about poor people sharing if nobody else does it.'

Arthur was known to have strong views on the question of sharing.

'It's more that people who don't have much probably understand that others need help, and so they're better at sharing. It's not a rule as such – it's called a proverb. A sort of short saying that helps you to remember what's important.'

'But I thought buffaloes were boys? Don't they have horns?'

'You can have male or female buffaloes. At least I think you can,' said Panenka, uncertainly. 'You have buffalo mozzarella, which comes from buffalo milk, so yeah: they can be male or female.'

'What about buffalo wings?'

'They're not from buffaloes. They're from chickens.'

'Anyway, what date are we at?'

'We haven't finished March – are you sure you want to do all these? It's going to take a while.'

Back in January, Marie-Thérèse had given Arthur a calendar from work, one of those where you tore off a page each day.

Arthur was a bit behind and Panenka was helping him to catch up, reading the pocket wisdom that was printed on each date. So far, Arthur was unimpressed by the thinkers of antiquity.

'Let's do a few more,' said Arthur with lukewarm enthusiasm.

'"Whoever seeks cake loses his bread" – what do you think about that Arthur?'

Arthur squinted in thought.

'I can live with that,' he said.

'Right, the next one: "Praise the day at sunset."'

'Aren't there any *useful* sayings in this calendar?' asked Arthur in frustration. 'Actual good advice that people can follow?'

'Like what?'

'Like in movies, if you're at a campfire at night, don't go off to kiss your girlfriend in the woods because that's how they get you.'

Panenka had to concede that it was wise in its way.

'Or, if you get caught doing something wrong,' Arthur continued, 'always say you didn't do it, because you can always change your answer later – but if you admit it straight away, you're stuck with that.'

'Maybe that's enough wisdom for now,' said Panenka, lifting the pile of raggedy paper squares. 'The recommended dose is one saying per day, and we've already done a few weeks' worth. We don't want to get too clever too suddenly – we might get a headache.'

It was out before he could stop himself saying it.

Now that he was seven, Arthur was at the age of ripening self-consciousness; the phase when children begin to notice that the world has not been made perfectly. It marks the point when a child goes from being a creature of their energy to something more tidal. In a good mood, he was a transparent, in-the-moment force; but when his spirits were low, everything became less readable. Panenka had spent the day tracing in Arthur's expressions and reactions any residue of the drama with the Iron Mask. There was something in the way that Arthur tugged Marie-Thérèse's sleeve earlier that morning, when she was leaving for work, which betrayed his anxiety about being left alone with his grandfather.

'Arthur?'

Panenka started stroking Arthur's eyebrows.

'I'm sorry about the other night. For giving you a fright.'

'Oh, okay.'

'And for taking your cheesy breadsticks.'

'I don't mind. I swap them in school anyway.'

'Is there anything you want to ask me about it? About my headache I mean.'

'Like what?'

Panenka realised he was close to deep water.

'You know, anything.'

There was a piece of fluff on Arthur's long eyelashes. Panenka picked it off.

'Mama does this too,' said Arthur after a while.

'Does what?'

'Whenever I'm relaxing, when it's quiet, she starts asking me serious things.'

'Do you not like that?'

'It's sneaky.'

'I suppose it is. But I also wanted to say thanks for looking after me. It was a nice thing to do.'

'Did you know that the brain can't feel pain?' said Arthur. 'I saw a video where they drilled into a man's head with, like, a pizza cutter, and operated on his brain while he was still awake. The doctor could make him move his hand and everything. So if you get one of those it won't hurt your brain? Don't be worried, okay?'

Arthur reached up and stroked Panenka's forehead, presumably where he thought the pain was located.

'Thanks, my friend. I won't.'

The key turned in the front door and Panenka could hear voices. Arthur rolled off the seat and ran out into the hall.

'Oh, thanks for the lovely hug, buddy. You're so good,' said Marie-Thérèse.

Panenka heard a familiar voice behind her.

'Hello, what's your name?' asked the voice.

'Arthur, of course.'

They were brought to the front room by Arthur dragging Marie-Thérèse's wrist, like a coupled train carriage, Esther following.

'Hi,' she said.

'Hey,' said Panenka. 'What a nice surprise.'

She stood there in her light camel coat, a look on her face that told him she'd been fully briefed on things.

'Grab your jacket, Arthur – guess what?' said Marie-Thérèse. 'I spoke to Daddy and he said we could call over and go out for pancakes as a special treat, all three of us.'

'Can't Pop come?' asked Arthur.

'I'll go next time,' said Panenka.

Arthur grabbed his jacket and assaulted his grandfather with a hug at belly level. He addressed Esther sideways-on without eye contact: 'Hi/bye.'

'It was nice to meet you, Esther,' said Marie-Thérèse, brushing Arthur's hair with her fingers. 'Good luck with your barbershop – maybe I'll bring this fella there sometime. Dad – we'll be back at bedtime.'

The cheerful goodbyes were belied by her expression, a look conveying complicated things.

Esther hung up her coat and sat in the chair beside the couch where Panenka was still surrounded by proverbs. She was dressed in her barbershop black. No jewellery today.

'Don't you hate it when you get justifiably mad at someone and then it turns out not to be their fault?' she said. 'How is your head?'

'I haven't had any headaches since the other night. We'll have to wait and see what happens. Look, I'm sorry for not telling you. I was planning to say something, honestly, but–'

'How serious is all this?'

Panenka's face became overcast.

'What's your body telling you?' she tried again.

'It's bracing itself. At least that's how it feels.'

'It must be scary for you.'

'All I can see are the problems it causes. The mound of problems that it's adding to. But yes, the fear is there too. Always there. I can feel it underneath everything else.'

Panenka brushed a few crumbs from the arm of the chair.

'I just feel sorry about everything,' he said.

'Sorry for what?'

'It's hard to explain. Without realising it, I think I had always hoped that there would be something in my future that would fix my past. I was naïve enough to think there would always be enough time for that to happen. But then you get to a point – the point I'm at now – where all I can see is the shadow I'll leave behind me.'

He addressed his words to his thumbs, which pressed together until the tips of the nails turned white.

'But what have you done that's so bad, Joseph? How can you talk about yourself like that?'

'There's too much to explain.'

'Like what? Your marriage failed – you're human. You're doing your best with Marie-Thérèse and Arthur. Is this all because of a stupid football game? This ridiculous Panenka business? You made a mistake. So what? You were a kid. A young kid, that's all.'

His throat became swollen hearing her take his side. No one had ever done that. Not even he had done that.

'When you grow up somewhere,' he said, 'and when your world amounts to a group of people who are all connected to the same place, it's impossible to keep any sort of separation: the people, the town, Seneca, it all becomes one thing. There are lots of unhappy people here, and it's a huge relief for them to agree on a single cause of that unhappiness. Something they can understand and which costs them nothing.'

'It's so unfair on you though!' said Esther. 'How can you accept the impossible burden of a whole town's failures? That's unreasonable to the point of being sacrificial.'

He smiled, more in resignation that anything.

'Why did you do it anyway?' she asked. 'The Panenka, I mean. Like, if it's such a big deal and everything.'

The question hung in the air. The room seemed to fall still around it. A question that had been worn into the grain of his thoughts over many years. So much discussed by so many people and yet, strangely, he had never been asked it directly.

'It's hard to explain,' he said. 'I think I thought that everyone had been through so much in the town for so long that I wanted to create something beautiful for them. It wasn't about showing off or trying to be clever. I had no thought for myself at all. Maybe if I had thought of myself, and the risks, I'd never have done it. My coach, Cesar, had taught us to play with such a pure type of freedom. To play like children is what he said. I thought everyone deserved a special moment. Something that would make Seneca and its fans respect themselves again.'

'Maybe their reaction shows that they don't deserve beautiful moments,' she said.

'Believe me – I spent *years* telling myself the very same thing. It feels like I spent my whole adult life that way, alone with my own grief about it all. But that stuff is such slow poison.'

Panenka gathered up the crumpled proverbs and tossed them on the table full of toys.

'How long did this all go on?' she asked.

'People talk about it even now. Everyone still knows me as Panenka. I decided that if I didn't fight against people calling me that, accepted it even, then everything would stop with me and I would own it. That way of looking at things appeals to you when you're obsessed. You become captured by your obsession. Maybe with Seneca doing well again, people will move on, but I'm not so sure. This town is a stubbornly traditional place. People are slow to let go of things.'

These were some of his oldest words, yet he had never said them aloud until now. He could feel his jaw quiver as he saw their effect on her. Tears collected in his eyes, so weary and sad.

'You must have had incredible strength to keep you going, though? Doesn't that give you some self-belief?' she asked.

'For so long I was afraid to stay close to anybody because I had so much anger and confusion inside me. I knew that I couldn't let anyone into my life until all that had passed. The problem I could never solve was how to relate to people in the meantime. Other people's love is frightening when you're suffering. It's overwhelming. When you're consumed with the effort of processing internal pain, it becomes impossible to do anything else. It's like holding your breath under water: you realise that you need to breathe but if you breathe at the wrong time, you drown. I only survived thanks to the people in my life – people I repaid by letting them down. So that's how it has been... And then I met you.'

'And then you met me.'

Now it was Esther's eyes that became misty.

'You saw through me straight away,' he said. 'You saw *into* me before you even knew me. There was something about you that cut through all that heavy, soupy history and snapped me back to now, woke me up again. Maybe unhappy people have a way of finding each other but, whatever the explanation, I am so, so glad it happened. I love you very, very much, Esther, but I don't know what's ahead for me. I would dearly love to have you in my life, if only you hadn't come so late. It wouldn't be fair to invite you into whatever happens next. How could I do that to someone I care about this much?'

He wanted her to see him as he saw himself. For her to understand what she meant to him. He had known it was love from the first moment he had felt her heart beat stronger than his own, and knew that he would do anything not to break it.

'Listening to you feels like I've walked in on the last five minutes of a movie,' she said. 'I'm not sure I could ever truly make sense of everything you've gone through, but the essence of what you're saying isn't foreign to me. I know what it's like to go through something that bends the story of your past to make it look like it was always leading to that one point, corrupting everything that went before. And the future? The future turns out to be a kite crashed in the sand. For you it was Seneca, for me it was Eugene.'

The room had dimmed while they were talking, too gradually for them to notice.

'But whatever is lost, something else always grows back in its place. A big tree falls in a storm, a hundred-year-old tree that's utterly irreplaceable, and yet when the tree goes, so does its shade. And when it's gone, there's light for the first time and something different grows back in its place. Or maybe for a while there is just space, and a new way of looking at things. There's no philosophy in that – no *answers.* Just a new starting point and a quiet letting go of what's already gone.'

Everything she said sounded new and yet familiar to him. In other words, true.

'Joseph,' she said, in an emboldened voice. 'I think we agreed, didn't we, that our relationship is something different. I think we both said that and meant it, even if we hadn't yet found the words to explain what we meant. But what *I* think it means is that we're free to love each other in whatever way that love comes to us. We may be dented and perhaps unfixable, but so what? Having found each other, isn't that miraculous enough? Don't shut down, Joseph. Please. Don't close yourself off. I'll be honest. I'm scared for you, and scared for myself, that something is already taking you away from me. But isn't that what allowing yourself be loved is all about – letting something greater than fear into your life?'

Panenka lifted his gaze to look at Esther, and saw that her face held what little light was left in the room.

# Chapter 29: Saint Teresa's Cathedral

The town had always been slow-starting, and the best time to see it was in early morning when the buildings stood by themselves, their seriousness offset by their stillness. Joseph had arranged to meet Esther at the newspaper kiosk near the cathedral. In the days since their last meeting, when he had finally opened the vault of his life to her, there had been other minor attacks of the Iron Mask but there had also been a settling of life's sediment. The resulting clarity felt new.

Marie-Thérèse took some persuading that moving back into her old apartment with Arthur was still the right thing to do; having finally been brought close to her father, the distance seemed unsafe to her. But their relationship felt level and whatever they couldn't bridge by certainty would have to be bridged by trust, both now and from now on; and anyway, Vincent would be staying with him for a while, so there was that.

Her relationship with Vincent had entered a new phase and, though they were both still tender from the wound, there was healing also, with Arthur its main agent. They were making an effort again, inching towards a consensual peace as separate people, and away from the burden of obligatory love. Vincent, well, Vincent had some thinking to do. In the meantime he would keep himself occupied with the grand plan that he announced to his customers at the café-bar: namely, that he would keep things as they were and always had been.

Esther arrived and paid for the newspaper Joseph was reading.

'You can buy the coffee,' she said.

'There's something I want to show you first.'

'Oh, sure – a surprise before coffee,' she said. 'That's a bit of a gamble.'

'It won't take long. Come on.'

Joseph led her across the square in the direction of Saint Teresa's, a gigantic and ornate gothic masterpiece, now sooty and shadowed from the town's traffic pollution, its face veiled in scaffolding and green mesh for its restoration. The central doorway stood like a giant pipe organ, the heavy wooden door itself decorated with figures from the saintly to the grotesque, honouring – or, if not honouring, then remembering – those who had lived parable lives. Joseph removed a complicated set of labelled keys from his jacket and pressed his index finger to his lips. Esther complied and left her piqued curiosity unexpressed.

Once inside, Joseph closed the heavy wooden door gently and locked it. There were already a few people in the cathedral: workers in hard hats and hi-vis vests, nobody clerical.

'Well, this is exciting,' whispered Esther. 'Are we allowed in here?'

'I wanted you to see where I work.'

Esther mimed a visibly-impressed 'O,' her face opening with surprise.

'What is it you do? I know you like to keep things private, but if you tell me you're some sort of priest or monk or something, I'm going to squeal.'

'No, nothing like that. I work up there,' he said, pointing above their heads.

'Doing what exactly?'

'You see that window? The large round one with all the colours? It's called a rose window, or you could call it a Catherine window.'

'Did you restore that?'

'Sort of. I'm responsible for cleaning it. We have to do it all slowly and carefully. I've been working on it for the past couple of weeks. I've been doing all these windows for months now.'

'You're a window cleaner,' she said to herself, trying to reconcile the exotic and the mundane that was packed into the explanation.

'I'm actually a conservation specialist – you were supposed to be impressed. I had to get accredited and everything.'

'Tell me, what do you clean it with?'

'Cotton buds.'

'You mean the little things I use for my ears?'

'It's not safe to put them in your ears – it says so on the box – but yes, those. And deionised water.'

'Why deionised – what's wrong with ions?'

'We have to be extra careful. Do you want to have a look? I've cleared it with my boss.'

'Which one's your boss?'

'That's her over there on the stepladder, wearing the fleece.'

'A young lady boss! What is she – thirty? Aren't you all unexpectedly modern!' Esther teased.

'She knows this cathedral better than anybody – she's overseeing the restoration pane by pane, stone by stone. And she's been very understanding – everybody likes her.'

'I have to say, I never pictured you doing something like this. Conservation. And you a footballer.'

'I know. I love it though. I get into this zone of concentration and detail and lose myself. It's painstaking – every day you go home and think nothing has improved, but then when you stand back and look at how it has changed over time, everything is so much brighter.'

'Maybe now I understand why it suits you,' she said, looking at him and taking him in.

'Here – you need to wear one of these,' he said, handing her a yellow hard hat. 'Do you mind ladders?'

'Yes, but I'll follow you. This is such a treat.'

They climbed up to the first platform of the scaffold, Esther gripping the rungs nervously.

'If I were to do this again, I'd bring different footwear,' she said, regretting her musketeer boots.

They stood at the top, the platform steady but not without a little unsettling movement. The light that came through the rose window formed a kaleidoscope on their faces. He looked at Esther, bathed in purples and reds and golds and blues and a million other pixels of gothic colour.

'This is spectacular,' she said softly, holding her hand close to the window without touching it, as if the light itself were tactile.

'It's a nice view over the cathedral too, if you look this way,' said Joseph, guiding her over to the guardrail that overlooked the empty chamber, decorated by the light of the rose window behind them. Rows of wooden pews were organised for worship under a vaulted ceiling; a room of histories and symbols; an encyclopaedia in glass and stone.

'It's safe, I promise. I spend every day up here,' he said offering her his hand.

Esther eased herself slowly beside him, not wanting to go too close to the barrier.

'This is nice,' she said. 'A little terrifying, but nice.'

'Very few people have ever had the chance to see the cathedral from this perspective,' he said. 'Through the eye of the rose window. It reminds me of the way you look at the world. Everything is so different and so beautiful. That's why I wanted to show it to you.'

'It's truly something else,' she said, linking her arm around his and resting her cheekbone on his shoulder.

They sank into the peace of the moment and stood together silently, the cathedral receiving their gaze.

Esther turned to share something she had noticed, but saw that Joseph was tracing a thought inside himself.

'What is it?' she asked.

'You know, if I had a choice... If I could choose an ending,' he said quietly, 'this would be it. Here with you, your face stained by the light.'

'Don't make me cry, Joseph.'

'Never, Esther. I never would.'

# Acknowledgements

I couldn't have written this book without the help, support and encouragement of my loving wife, Sinéad. I love you with all my heart, always.

Thanks to Kevin and Hetha Duffy and everyone at Bluemoose Books for your faith in me and for affording me the creative freedom to express my imagination. Your hard work, vision and commitment to independent publishing are an inspiration.

My sincere thanks to my editor Lin Webb for your meticulous care and attention, and for your sensitivity to the emotional lives of these characters. You always make me want to do my best for readers.

I am indebted to Leonora Rustamova at Bluemoose Books for your perceptive reading of the manuscript and for your helpful comments on it.

I am truly grateful for the feedback I received throughout the writing process from my dear friend Mike Stevens, who remains a constant source of support and a sounding board for all my doubts.

Special thanks to my friend Helen Vassallo, whose insightful comments on Panenka came at a time when my writing and my confidence needed it.

My thanks and appreciation to Brendan Crowley, of the All Sports Book Reviews blog, for your careful reading of the manuscript and for providing helpful feedback on the football sections in particular. I would like to state definitively for the record that Brendan, who reads sports biographies almost exclusively, was not the inspiration for Andrew in Leonard and Hungry Paul.